SHOWDOWN WITH A CHEAT!

"Mayo!" cried Mr. Morrissey.

As he spoke, people dived to get away from possible flying bullets. They had barely sufficient time. Morrissey was revealed with his rifle at his shoulder and his forefinger curled upon the trigger. At the touch of his voice, as though operated by a spring, Tommy Mayo whirled...

Speed could never have saved Tommy, taken as he was from behind. But as he whirled he leaped sidewise. At the same instant, Tommy turned, and his revolver was in his hand. Even before most people had seen the flash of it they heard the report.

Then they saw Morrissey reel, fumble before him, and go down on one knee. There had been time for Tommy to follow his first shot with three more—but he stood with his revolver hanging at his side, watching the other. And what he saw was Morrissey jerking the rifle to his shoulder once more, as he kneeled in the dust of the street!

Warner Books by
MAX BRAND

THE
MAKING
OF A
GUNMAN

Max Brand

WARNER BOOKS

A Warner Communications Company

Originally published in *Western Story Magazine* under the title
Western Tommy, written under the pseudonym of David Manning.

WARNER BOOKS EDITION

Warner Books, Inc.
666 Fifth Avenue
New York, N.Y. 10103

 A Warner Communications Company

Printed in the United States of America

First Warner Books Printing: October, 1984

10 9 8 7 6 5 4 3 2 1

1

When Harry Grant came to find his friend, Jack Mayo, he found him changed beyond expectation. It was fifteen years or more since Grant had seen the other. Jack had been a rough, good-natured, brown-faced miner, as ready to drink up his wages on Saturday night as any other man could be.

In the obscure offing there had been a family. It was left behind in one of the villages away from the mountains, and Harry Grant remembered that his friend used to send money home after a successful session at poker. Families did not bother mountaineers much in those days.

But Jack Mayo had changed a great deal. Grant had not traveled ten miles through the old country before he was aware of the change, though of its extent he could not be sure. He only knew that when he said "Jack Mayo," men opened their eyes at him and instantly pointed out the way.

Women, when he asked the road to the Mayo house, would pause to look at him with interest, before they answered. Even the children on the road from school smiled and instantly gave him directions.

Harry Grant became more thoughtful, as he kept his horse

1

going. He was a man of thoughtful nature. He had a lean, intelligent face; his eyes were reflective. His smile even was abstracted and meditative. As he rode, he kept his eyes straight before him, down the trail.

From the breast pocket of his coat he took a long morocco case, and when he had opened this carefully with his lean fingers, he picked out a cigar, long and dark and narrow. He lighted it with much care. Foolish smokers merely touch a match to the end of a cigar; the wise man makes sure that the fire covers the end of the tobacco leaves in a complete circle. Harry Grant stopped his horse for this ceremony of lighting the cigar.

Then he went on, with the cigar held firmly between his teeth exactly in the middle of his mouth, and smoking deliberately—just fast enough to keep the fire well spread out in the tobacco. This required, indeed, much skill. For there are many rates of puffing needed as an accomplishment. He who smokes indoors with skill may be an amateur in the open air. But Harry Grant was perfect in any surroundings.

He rode on, enjoying to the uttermost every particle of solace that was to be found in the Havana. Finally he came to the top of a hill which overlooked a neat little valley, that had been dropped comfortably into the lap of a mountain. It was two miles in length, perhaps, and a quarter of that distance in breadth; there were some three or four hundred acres of land—some pastured, but most of it under close cultivation.

In the midst of this happy valley, with two flashing brooks running across it, there was a broad white house clustered around by tall trees. This was the place, then, as he had heard it described some score of times in the last thirty miles. For he had paused often on purpose, to make out by the tones of the speakers and the expression of their faces what their inward thoughts of Mr. Jack Mayo might be.

He sat the saddle, motionless, for a time on the top of the hill. Presently he removed the cigar from his teeth and held it in the fingers of his gloved hand—so exquisitely gloved, however, that the softest and the most delicate kid never clad the slender hand of a girl so perfectly as did this glove fit the hand of Mr. Harry Grant. He spoke aloud, to the ears of his mare, who canted her head a little to one side with an absurd air of listening to him.

"What has happened to Jack Mayo, Dolly?" he asked. How absurd did that name of frills and flounces sound in the midst of the mountains, the big, iron mountains! Dolly! "What has happened to Jack Mayo? Has he settled down as firmly as the house he has built? Has he become as stupid and as—"

He paused, replaced the cigar between his teeth with a smile, and rode on down the hill.

The moment he came into the valley, the road changed to a well-arched surface, heavily graveled—perhaps with a rock foundation, to judge by the smallness of the ruts. He went by well-built fences, with not a board loose, and not a length of wire down. It was spring. Half the valley was black with the spring plowing, and yonder in a hundred-acre field two eight-mule gang plows were working at two big lands into which the field had been split.

There was rich soil, everywhere. A forest had once grown here, and out of leaf mold, decayed roots, and disintegrated stumps, that soil had been composed. The keen eye of Harry Grant probed the value of this ground. Yonder a man was driving a seeder over a plowed field, now a dull gray from the drying sun. The seed swished out like a fine spray of water; and behind the sower came the broad harrows, dragged by a twelve-mule team.

Here was prosperity, to be sure. Harry Grant took stock of it all; he took stock, also, of the distance between the ranch in the valley and the nearest shipping point. He calculated all of this, and then he estimated the value of that land. A hundred and fifty dollars an acre—no, at a most moderate guess, he could say that it was worth a hundred dollars per acre. That would be thirty or forty thousand dollars in land, then.

The mules, the plows, the new-painted sower wagon, the

good harness on the livestock—all told of great prosperity. Yes, if it were not for the great distance to the railroad, that fine land would be worth two hundred dollars an acre, if it were worth a cent, without mentioning the orchard lands, nearer to the house, and the truck gardens in the fine soil on the banks of the creeks.

Harry Grant revised his estimate upward. The owner of this farm had a property which could not be valued, probably, at less than a hundred thousand dollars, by the time rolling stock, livestock, house, outbuilding, barn, and all the little trappings of a ranch were considered. And if transportation were easier, it was worth twice that amount!

What Mr. Harry Grant said to himself, as he viewed all of this prosperity at closer hand, was: "He can stand trimming. Oh, he can stand quite a bit of it."

He did not laugh as he said this; he never laughed. But there was a faint wrinkling at the corners of his mouth, and his eye lightened a shade. He took off his cap—an odd thing to see a man in the West wearing a cap on horseback—and he smoothed his hair. With that glossy black hair covered, his lean face, weathered and sun stained, looked his full fifty years. With the black hair showing, he seemed a scant forty. Perhaps the truth was about a halfway point between the two. Then he settled the cap upon his head once more and jogged Dolly toward the ranch house.

The driver of the plow team in the next field stopped and gaped as he saw the stranger. For one in that country would have to travel far to see a man like Harry Grant, with his little English saddle, his short stirrup leathers, and his neatly fitted riding trousers. He could have fitted into an English landscape. Such a picture was not intended for the giddy sweep and the wild expanse, the carelessness of a Western mountain desert.

Harry Grant did not turn his head toward the staring plowman. He simply held on his way, pausing at nothing, missing nothing, until he crossed the two strong bridges which arched the brooks, one after the other. Beneath the lower side of the second bridge he saw a little landing place, and at the landing there was a small, blunt-ended flatboat capable of carrying five or six tons. Again Harry Grant revised his estimate upward. If there was water transportation for the products of the farm, then, indeed, the land was worth more—much more!

He was among the little buildings which bordered the ranch house. They spread out from it like sticks from the handle of a fan—no, rather like a ring attached to a staple. Side by side, but swinging in a circle, there was a group of little cottages. Around each cottage was its own reserved plot of ground. All the space behind the houses was devoted to separate vegetable gardens—all the space on the inside of the circle, toward which the houses faced, was given over to a broad park, covered with a well-trimmed lawn, big trees here and there, patches of bright flowers, already beginning to bloom.

Through the center of the circle, the roadway drove straight up to the face of the ranch house itself. But the little houses which surrounded the parked place were not for adornment only. They contained also shops of various kinds. The hammer of the blacksmith was ringing, the smoke of his forge arose, and in the narrow yard behind his house there was a jumble of wreckage—broken-down wagons, heaped implements of agriculture under appropriate sheds.

There was the scream of the carpenter's saw and the rapid tapping of his hammer in the adjoining shop. Perhaps in each of the other houses near the great ranch house there were other men at work at varying handicrafts.

The pleasure of Harry Grant increased each moment, as he passed by these greater and greater signs of prosperity. One might have thought that it all added to his own possessions in this world, instead of belonging to another man. Finally, he came close under the front of the main building itself, and there he removed the slender black cigar from between his teeth and called out to a lumbering form, at that moment striding around the corner of the house:

"Jack Mayo! Jack Mayo!"

The big, bulky, awkward-stepping man floundered in midstride. Then he braced himself against the wall of the house and stared at the newcomer in speechless emotion.

2

By the time Jack Mayo recovered himself, Harry Grant was off his horse. He did not seem to hurry, but he was on the ground instantly, the bridle reins tucked under his arm, his riding crop with the reins, and the glove drawn from his right hand. With his faint smile Grant advanced slowly to meet the big man.

But Jack Mayo came like a gigantic child, whooping and leaping, throwing his hands up in the air and laughing with joy. He crushed Harry Grant in great, loose, powerful arms. Then he began to pump the hand and arm of his old friend.

"Oh, Harry—ain't it good to see you? Ain't it good to see you?"

Harry Grant said: "How did it happen?"

"It's my second wife," said Jack Mayo, instantly understanding what was meant.

"She owned all of this? Well, Jack you get a lot of credit for keeping it up in such tiptop shape!"

"Keep it up? Man—I done the work to make it what it is!"

"And still you keep as fat as this?"

"Look inside of my face, Harry. I'm gettin' fat now, because the work is done, and I got somebody to take the worry of the place off of my shoulders. Well, it's only two years back that I've been takin' it easy!''

"I understand," said Harry Grant. "I understand! She kept you hard at it?''

"When my wife, Nelly, died I was left sort of stranded, with nothin' but the kids on my hands and nothin' to do with 'em. I asked a couple of girls to marry me. When they turned me down the matter was sifted down to Mary. I went to Mary and asked her to marry me.

" 'What you got in the way of a home?' asks Mary.

"I had been drinking, and I was pretty well plastered by that time. Yep, I owned about half the mountains, by my way of thinking, and I told Mary what I thought. I laid it on pretty thick. First she began doubting me. But after awhile I laid it on so thick that she wasn't sure. Finally she believed me! She thought I was simply tight and was throwing myself away.

"Well, that was the first millionaire in disguise that ever was throwed at the head of Mary, and she didn't waste no time. She got me to a preacher so quick my head swam, and before I knew it, I was spliced all proper.

"The minute that I was married, she began to take me in hand—not hard—just easy. She got me sobered up in record time and then she came home with me. Well, when I pulled up in front of the shack, she give me one look and seen through the whole dodge. But she didn't bust out cryin'. She sat up stiff with her head in the air and didn't say nothing.

"I took her into the house and left her to look around and see how bad things was. Then I sloped over to the neighbor's and brought back the boys. When she seen them she pressed her lips together, but that was all that she done. She didn't say a word to them, except: 'You and me are gunna get better acquainted, a lot.' Then she turns on me and says: 'And you and me'll get better acquainted, too, husband!'

"That was how she started with me. I wasn't no millionaire, and she seen it quick enough. But she started tryin' to make out of me the thing that I started pretending to be. She started me after the money, that I had lied about, and she never left the whip off my back until I was wore out and took sick, about two year back!''

At the thought of the long struggle, and the long torment, Jack Mayo fell sadly silent.

"And now you have four hundred acres of fine land!" said Harry Grant.

"I got a thousand," said Jack Mayo without joy. "All you can see is the lower valley, where I started the ranch first. But the best of the land is beyond the turn of the hills, up yonder. I got more'n six hundred acres up there."

"You have a hundred and fifty thousand dollars' worth of land, in land alone!"

Jack Mayo looked at his companion in silent thought. "Well," said he at last, "you're as much of a farmer as I was when Mary took me in hand. No, son, this here land ain't ordinary common or garden land. This here land is the kind that calls less than twelve sacks of wheat to the acre a poor crop. That's the kind of a crop that it puts out. Less than twenty-five sacks of barley is a failure in this valley.

"This here land is made up of nothin' but richness. All you got to do is give it a kick per acre and throw a handful of seed into it, and it pours out wheat by the sack. Careless farming wouldn't suit Mary. She does everything by improved methods!"

"It sounds like a fairy story," said Harry Grant, looking out over the beautiful valley with a brighter light than ever in his eye.

"A fairy story?" repeated Jack Mayo sourly. "Anyways, there's a witch in it! Well, sir, to begin with we got a wedge of this here land by luck. Just plain range, like the rest of the range. But my Mary could read the mind of a piece of ground plumb easy. She spaded up some of this ground and come back into the shack and throwed down a handful of worms. 'Where them things is, wheat'll grow,' says she.

"Right there was where my troubles all started. Right away I had to mortgage my soul to get an option on the whole valley and sell myself for a slave to get seed to sow only a part of the land. Well, sir, that crop was enough to choke you, it was so dog-gone big. And when I wondered how I could get that crop to the railroad, Mary had gone over the brooks and found where, by smoothing out a couple of rocky places and straightening a couple of mud-flat bends, we could send boats right down to town and the trains!

"Well, sir, the rest was easy. Three crops bought the land and built us a house. Three more crops gave us all the improvements that you can see. And now for eight years we been carting money galore to the bank."

"Money in the bank!" echoed Harry Grant.

"Aye," nodded Jack Mayo. "Lots and lots of it! Nigh onto two hundred thousand dollars in the bank. And three hundred thousand more wouldn't buy the valley off me."

"Before Mary ends," said Harry Grant, "she'll have you the millionaire that you pretended to be at the first."

"I suppose she won't let up till she's done it," said Jack Mayo.

"I congratulate you, Jack."

But Jack overlooked the extended hand. "What sort of fun is it for me?" he asked sourly.

"You're not happy?"

"The devil—no!"

"With a million in sight?"

"I've spent a million minutes in Hades to get it. The million minutes that I could of been lazyin' in the sun, or fishin' or huntin', or swappin' lies with the boys and growing up and having a general good, useless sort of a time all around—and watching the sun and smelling the wind—and doing nothing.

"Well, sir, that's what I've give up to get this here valley and a bank account for somebody else to use and enjoy when I'm dead. No, sir, there ain't a part of this valley that really belongs to me. It's her work. I'm just one of the hands that she's been using. And I hate the sight of this cursed valley!"

"Pain makes the philosophic mind," said Harry.

"What?"

"Nothing."

"And now about yourself."

"Well, to begin with, I haven't a million, or the half of it!"

"Ah, but you have enough, Harry! I can tell by the odor of tobacco and by the look of your clothes. I never wore clothes like that! And by the look of your hoss, most of all. Dog-gone me if that mare ain't a jim-dandy, old son! How much did you pay for her?"

Harry chuckled. "The last check that bought her," said he, "was for twenty-five hundred dollars."

"Twenty-five hundred! Suffering cats!" gasped Jack.

He walked all around Dolly in admiration which was as serious as alarm would be. "I believe it," said he at last. "My, my, what a price for a hoss! But like settin' on a dog-gone blowin' cloud, I suppose, to ride her?"

"Yes."

"And fast as the wind, I s'pose?"

"Yes, pretty fast."

"Wait till I call Mary to look at her. Hey, Mary—hey, Tommy; hey, Frank, come swarmin' out here, because I want you to have a look at a hoss that's a hoss—yes, sir, a hoss that is sure a real hoss!"

His voice rose and swelled and seemed to fill the valley from mountain to hill. There were dim answers from within the house. Then the front door flew open, and out stepped a little, erect woman in an ugly brown dress with her head stiffly in the air, her features as cleanly cut and as hard as the features of a Roman statue. Behind her there walked forth two big young men, who stayed discreetly to the rear while she went down the steps.

3

It was impossible to look at those two young men, though they were worth enough attention. All that could be seen was the face of Mary Mayo. She came down, and her lean fingers clasped the lean fingers of Harry Grant.

"I've heard a lot of talk about you," said she. "But I didn't have no sort of a picture of you in my mind. Of course, it's fine for Jack to have you. Have you met our boys?"

The boys stepped forward—one was a big, brawny-shouldered, lean-cheeked boy with Herculean torso and a clear, good-natured eye.

"This is Frank Mayo."

Frank shook hands with a word and passed on. And a sleek-faced youth took his place; not so tall as Frank, not so wide of shoulder by far—very long and light of foot and hand, a little too fat—with dull, sleepy, brown eyes.

"This is Tommy. Stand straight, Tommy! Can't you stand up and shake hands like a man?"

After all, Tommy was twenty-one—and he certainly appeared to be far beyond the age when a man receives such words from anyone. But he did not appear to hear. He did not alter his slouching attitude. Not the slightest light came into his dull, brown eyes. His handclasp was as flaccid as butcher's meat. He lounged on away from Harry Grant, and he was followed by a glance of fire from his stepmother.

Sometimes Harry Grant made up his mind very quickly. But now he was a little bewildered, and he cast a sharp look after that second boy, saying to himself: "Deaf, or a half-wit, or—"

"And look, Mary," said Jack Mayo, "at the sort of a hoss that old Harry comes riding, will you? She ain't so bad, is she? Could a man get along with a hoss like that for riding on? Yes, I reckon that maybe he could get along, all right! Oh, yes, he could get along! Would you guess how much this here little mare cost, Mary?"

Mary walked gravely around the mare with her cold, strong hands lightly clasped together. Opposite the left foreleg she stopped, paused, and ran her fingers lightly over the knee, before and behind. Then she looked sidewise at Mr. Grant. She did not smile, but Mr. Grant did.

"Very well," said Mary Mayo. "I dunno how much she cost, but I guess it was a lot. Too much, perhaps!"

"Try any hoss on the ranch against her," said Jack Mayo sharply. "How can you say it was too much for that hoss when you ain't even heard—"

"Can this mare be used for cutting?" asked Mary.

"No," said Grant, "it can't be used for cutting cattle."

"Or riding herd, or anything else on a ranch?"

"It has no training for that."

"Well!" said Mary. "Come inside and rest yourself, Mr. Grant. I hope your hoss is a right-down easy-ridin' hoss, though."

"I like her very well," said Mr. Grant. "She has a peculiar value to me."

"How?" asked Mary.

"I have very bad nerves," said Mr. Grant. "I cannot stand a rough-gaited horse, and Dolly goes like running water."

"Dolly?" repeated Mary, and she looked again from the

grim face of little Mr. Grant to the beautiful mare. "Well!" said she. "Come inside and rest yourself, will you?"

"I'd like to stay outside for a little and look over your ranch. It seems to be a huge place—and beautifully kept!"

"It's something; it's something," said Mrs. Mayo impatiently. "If one could get men to work at things and manage things—but those hills could be worked with a little terracing. Two hundred acres of farmland turned over to grazing, it looks to me! Besides, what's in the insides of those hills and this here mountain? Do we know? We do not know! Nobody has prospected 'em. And how far up the valley could we get more land, and more land? We can't tell yet! I can't be everywhere—and the men—oh, we got a little start, here, and that's all that I can say!"

She could not stay any longer. There was work in the house that needed her attention, and off she went.

"Gets to bed at twelve," said Jack Mayo in a hoarse aside of admiration and terror and wonder, as she moved away, "gets up at five. Starts in work. Keeps doin' cookin' and housework till ten."

"Housework!" exclaimed Grant.

"She's tried servants. But they don't keep very well up here with Mary. She teaches 'em too much, I guess. After ten she's ready for other things. She throws up two other meals a day for us, of course. But she does 'em slick and quick. She's a fast mover. The rest of the time, till twelve at night—well, she's doin' accounts and makin' out plans and writing checks and sending out letters for business. She's got herself a typewriter so's she could write her letters faster.

"At first that typewriter used to go with a hitch step. But then it got along so's she could make it purr like a cat. Every last day of her life, she climbs onto a saddle and takes a whirl clean around these here acres of hers—ours, I mean. She rides all around the place, and no matter how hard and how careful everybody works, she can always find at least six things that's going wrong. There ain't nobody exactly like her, old-timer, and you can lay to that!"

To all of this explosion, Mr. Grant listened with a quiet attention, and in the meantime, he was walking with his old companion toward the stable. There he put up the mare. With his own hands he rubbed her down and saw to the feeding of her.

"And what might you be doing, Harry, vacationing?"

"You might call it that. Nervous, though. The strain of business rather tells on a man, after a time. I came out West to travel over some of the old trails."

"But what business, Harry?"

"Broker, Jack."

"Broker?"

"I work between people and the things that they want. I'm a middleman. I get little commissions here and there. Take them altogether, they work up to a tidy income."

"Ah," said Jack Mayo, "there wasn't never no doubt that you'd always be prosperous—and free, Harry, free!"

Harry Grant changed the subject. "You have two sons, Jack," said he.

"Aye. One of 'em is such a fine fellow that it makes me happy just to think of him. And one of 'em is poison mean and worthless."

"That's—"

"Tommy, of course. There ain't nobody like him. You know that I ain't the hardest man in the world to please when it comes to working. I sort of *like* to see a boy lazy and take it easy. It sort of worries me to see the way that Frank gets up at five in the morning, all the same as Mary, and the way he goes, all through the day. But this here Tommy—why, what's he good for? He can't read a book without goin' to sleep. He can't ride a hoss without gettin' bucked off. He can't do a day's work without gettin' blistered hands, or something like that, and then he comes into the house and takes a month getting rid of troubles.

"Start Tommy at work for one day, and he develops enough troubles to bring the doctor here once a day for a month. Sometimes he gets his liver clean out of whack.

Sometimes he gets his heart upset. The doctor don't know what to make of him. Well, even Mary give it up at last. She's got the strongest will in the whole darn world, and I'm right here to say so! But she ain't strong enough to budge Tommy! No, sir, he can sleep harder than she can work!''

Rage, disgust, scorn, and despair were all in the voice of Jack Mayo.

"This Frank of yours," said Harry Grant, "is a brave fellow, too, I suppose?"

"Oh, sure. There ain't nothin' that he wouldn't tackle!"

"And a straight-shooting boy, too?"

"It's a right pleasure to see him work with a rifle, old-timer. And it sure is fun to see him make a six-gun hop. Conversation from the hip—well, he can talk that way. He's a fine, upstanding boy, Grant. Take the opposite of everything that his good-for-nothing brother is, and you'll find that Frank is that. That's why he's so fine!"

"And he killed Conrad Black on top of the rest of his virtues, Jack. I envy you for your son more than I do for your fine ranch, I can tell you!"

"He killed Conrad Black? Frank has too much sense to get mixed up in a killing!"

"It wasn't Frank, then?"

"Him? Does he look like a killer?"

"But it was one of your boys, wasn't it?" asked Grant, frowning suddenly. "Have I ridden all the—Wasn't it one of your boys? Is there another Mayo family in this neighborhood?"

"It was one of my boys, of course. It was the good-for-nothing one, Tommy!"

"Ah!"

"Well?"

"I was wrong," said Grant, more to himself than to the other. "Not deaf—not half-witted, but—"

"What the devil are you talking about?"

"Tommy."

"And what about him?"

"There's a good deal to the man who killed Conrad Black."

"Bah!" snorted the incredulous father. "I know what you're thinking, but I tell you that it was all a chance. He met up with Conrad Black, when Con was drunk and foolish and reelin'. And he was mean enough to take a fight with Con, when he was half out of his head, like that. Even then, most likely Con would of killed the fool boy, except that his gun hung a mite when he started to draw it!"

"Did you know Conrad Black?"

"Everybody had heard tell of him, of course. I never met him."

"I knew him very well!"

"What of that?"

"Why," said Harry Grant, "nothing worth remarking, except that I'd like to have a little talk with this Tommy of yours."

4

They went slowly out from the stable. Jack Mayo was shaking his head slowly from side to side. "You were always a queer one, Harry," said he. "You could always see things where nobody else could see a trace. Well, what have you seen in Tommy?"

"You see," explained Harry Grant, "I have always known Con Black pretty well. I really know all about him, in fact."

"He was a bad one," Mayo nodded. "Everybody knew that. There wasn't any trial of Tommy, because folks was so glad to have that Black out of the way. However, it was a good thing that he was drunk."

"I remember about seven years ago," said Grant, "hearing about Conrad Black meeting the three men at the crossroads—"

"Barker, Cole, and Stevens. Sure. He killed two of 'em. And he left Stevens full of lead! That was a big day for Con Black. They acquitted him on that because they were pretty sure that one man wouldn't of started a fight with three, like that. But a lot of us was sure that Con Black was confident enough to tackle even three at a time!"

"And then to be snuffed out by a kid like Tommy Mayo!"

"It was the booze that beat Black."

"By the way, I understand that he was drinking pretty hard the day that he fought the three men at the crossroads."

"Sure. But not—"

He paused, for Harry Grant was smiling.

"What's up, Harry?" asked the rancher.

"Only this—I knew Con Black too well. And I know his *kind* too well. There was never a time in his life when he was as drunk as he pretended to be. There was never a time in his life when he was too drunk to fight well and make a quick draw."

"His gun hung," said Jack Mayo, frowning over this important piece of information.

"How do you know that it hung?"

"Because he was so slow in getting it out."

'Who said that?"

"The boys that were standing by."

"Maybe the boys didn't notice that it was the speed of Tommy and not the slowness of Conrad Black."

The rancher merely shook his head. "You've seen Tommy," he said, "and you ought to know better than that. There ain't nothin' fast about him. He ain't fast at one single thing, except sleep!"

"So much the better," said Harry Grant. "Perhaps he's saving his strength for a big day to come!"

"Tell that to Mary." The father grinned. "D'you aim to say that the killing of Con Black wasn't just a lucky accident?"

"Accidents like that don't happen! Bring out both of your sons, and I'll wager that Tommy will outshoot the big fellow—Frank!"

"Harry, are you wild? Ain't I seen them both shooting a hundred times?"

"Shooting for what?"

"Fun, or sport, of course."

"I'll hang up a better prize than that, and then you'll see a difference, old-timer!"

"What sort of a prize?"

"What will they like the most? I suppose that money means nothing to *your* boys, Jack."

"Don't it though! You don't figger on the way that Mary has raised them! Well, money means something to Frank, I mean. But not even money can get a rise out of Tommy. Plumb wasted ammunition is what that tramp is!"

"Hush!" said Harry Grant, holding up his hand.

There was a squeal of anger and then a snort from the barn, followed by a trampling of horse's hoofs.

"Someone is fooling around Dolly," snapped Grant, whirling about on his heel. "And she's a little tigress. I should have given a warning of that!"

He was off racing. Frightened Jack Mayo reached the barn a stride behind him. What they found was Dolly pricking her ears and sniffing eagerly at the face and the hair of Tommy Mayo, who sat in the manger before her, rubbing her nose and talking softly.

"What have you done to that mare, son?" asked Grant, frowning in wonder.

"Talking, as you see," said Tommy.

"It's a strange thing," said Grant. "She'll pay no attention to anyone but me, as a rule!"

"Aw," remarked the father, "I should of told you that he's got a sort of a way with horses—and dogs—when he wants to use it."

"You like the looks of that horse, Tommy?" asked Grant.

"Pretty fair," said Tommy.

He hung a loose arm over the neck of the man killer and stifled a yawn as he looked toward Grant with dull, dull eyes.

"Can't you speak up like a human bein'?" asked his father in a rage. "Ain't you got no more sense of respect for a gent like my old friend, Harry Grant?"

In place of answer, Tommy regarded Harry Grant from head to foot with the same lackluster eyes.

"The horse! The horse!" snapped Harry Grant, waving the reproof of his companion aside. "Tell me, Tommy, if you'd like to ride the mare?"

Tommy yawned again. "I guess that there ain't much chance," said he.

"If she ain't safe," said the father, "Tommy will fall off!"

"She's a raging devil with a stranger in the saddle," said Grant. "But would you like to try her, anyway?"

"Her?" said Tommy. "Raging devil? Oh, I guess not! Shall I saddle her up?"

"If you want to take the chance?"

"Chance?" queried Tommy.

He glided from the manger to the peg behind the mare where the saddle was hanging. He did not seem to move swiftly, but every touch accomplished magic wonders. The saddle dropped on the back of the mare; the cinches were quickly drawn up and tied. Then the bridle slipped upon the head of the mare, who parted her teeth willingly for the bit, strange to say!

In another moment the mare was in the open beyond the barn, and the boy was in the saddle. Dolly forgot her good manners of the stable. She plunged straight into the air with flattened ears and an angry squeal, which was echoed by Jack Mayo.

"Hey, Harry!" he yelled. "You'll be the death of that kid of mine. He'll be off in ten seconds!"

But ten seconds passed, and Tommy was still erect in the saddle. Indeed, he seemed to sit there at ease. And now, behold, he was laughing at them and waving one hand toward them.

"I'll be cursed!" said the father.

"You ought to be," Harry Grant chuckled. "Look at that! He's keeping her at that bucking with a spur in her flank! Did you say that boy couldn't ride?"

"He never—" began the father and then paused to gape as the mare tied herself into a wild knot in the air and landed with the force of a jarring hammer stroke.

Tommy laughed, while Grant said: "Man, man, did you ever give him a horse that he *wanted* to ride?"

Suddenly the antics of the mare ceased. She stopped short, and Tommy leaned over her neck, stroking it and speaking softly to her.

"He's taken the spur out of her," said Grant, still laughing to himself, "and now see her put up her ears—the little fool. Is that the stupid son you've been telling me about?"

Jack Mayo could think of no answer. He sought refuge in a liberal chew of tobacco.

Dolly was presently back in her stall, and Tommy came lounging out.

"Did you ever sit a better horse?" asked Grant.

"One," said Tommy.

"What?" cried the father. "A better than the mare?"

"Is Porter's Hagan a better horse?" asked Tommy.

"And you've rode Hagan?" asked the father with deep sarcasm.

"Once."

"What horse is that?" asked Grant. "Between you and me, I thought I was bringing the best horse into these mountains that had ever cantered here."

"I'll tell you," said Jack Mayo, "you've brought in the best usable one. But this here Porter has got that Hagan hoss that run wild for two years and run off so many hosses. Maybe you've heard tell? A three-quarter bred who escaped. They caught him—dropped with a bullet. They keep him inside of a corral with a nine-foot fence, and they use him for breeding. Only three men have had the nerve to even *try* to ride him."

"And you did?" Grant asked the boy.

Tommy leaned a long arm against the side of the barn and yawned again as he nodded. His head fell back a trifle. He was examining vacantly a bird that hopped about on the eaves above him.

"Him!" grunted the father. "*He* rode that tiger. Why, look at him, will you?"

Tommy Mayo did not change color under this burst of scorn. But straightening his body with a great effort, he dropped his hands into his trouser pockets and began to shamble away toward the house.

"You liked that Hagan pretty well, Tommy?" called Grant.

The boy stopped and, without turning his body, drawled over his shoulder: "Sure. Pretty well!"

"Turn around and try to act polite, will you?" cried the father. "My heavens, how Mary and me have tried to knock manners into the head of that young fool!"

"I mean to ask," said Grant, "if you would like to *have* the horse?"

Tommy turned with a faint grin. "Aw," said he, "I dunno that you get the point. That horse they hold for five hundred dollars flat. He's worth that much just for breeding. Can you imagine that?"

This remark of Tommy's was reenforced by the vigorous nodding of his father.

"Porter's Hagan," said he, "is worth a lot of money, in the eye of Porter. Them that want speed and looks should go to Porter's Hagan."

Mr. Grant was lighting a new cigar. When he had flicked away the match and watched it smolder on the ground until the last wisp of smoke had risen from it, he said: "Five hundred dollars is a rather neat price for a mountain horse. If I handed you five hundred dollars, would you go and spend it on that stallion?"

There was a faint glimmering in the eyes of the boy; he smiled without mirth. "I would do just that," he declared solemnly.

"Hark to him sing," said the father gloomily. "That's the sort of stuff that I got to listen to from him!"

"What would you do with him?" asked Harry Grant.

Tommy lifted his head, and his brown eyes searched the sky.

"Look yonder!" said he.

"Well?" asked Mr. Grant.

"D'you see that hawk?"

"I see it."

"Why don't you ask what it wants with wings?"

He looked up for another moment, his smile gradually dying. As he stood there, Mr. Grant surveyed him keenly—and the eye of Harry Grant, at that moment, was like the eye of a cattle buyer, when he glances at a type of the herd, or of a bargainer, when he looks into the face of a clever opponent. He saw all that was to be seen, until the flush died out of the face of Tommy, and his head fell, and his body, which had gained an inch or two of added stature during that upward glance, collapsed to its usual stature.

He was about to turn toward the house again, when Grant added quickly: "I would spend five hundred dollars, Mayo, to see which of your boys is the best shot."

Jack Mayo opened eyes and mouth at the same moment. But he shut his teeth again with a click.

"Don't be a fool!" he told his old friend. "I don't want to pick your pocket! I've told you already that Frank is a great hand with rifle or revolver and—"

"Wait a minute," said Tommy. "Did you say five hundred dollars?"

"I did," said Harry Grant.

"It's mine!" said Tommy, and he whirled and bolted for the house.

"Tell Frank!" called his father heavily.

He waved a hand above his shoulder and plunged into the house.

"He's fast on his feet, at least," said Harry Grant.

"I never saw him move like that before! I dunno what's happened to the kid. He's rattled. Because he knows that he can never beat Frank!"

"I don't!" said Grant.

"Harry, you're tempting me toward a bet, it looks like to me."

"I'll make the bet, if you want."

"Harry, I can't take the money, I've seen 'em shoot a hundred times. And Tommy can't hit the side of a barn."

"He's never had a reason to try hard," declared Grant. "I'll bet you a hundred."

"Why, if you want to throw away your money—two hundred, if you wish."

"Or three, Jack."

"I'll bet you four hundred, Harry."

"Five hundred even," suggested Grant. "If I lose—five hundred in your pocket, old-timer. If I win, you hand me the price of Porter's Hagan."

They shook hands on that, as Tommy and Frank came out of the house. Frank came as one would have expected—his head high, his strong face lighted, his step firm. He showed no exultation—only a firm and manly confidence.

"Rifle or revolver, Frankie?" asked Tommy. "What'll you try first?"

"My name is Frank," said the elder son. "I don't wear that other name, and you know it."

He favored Tommy with a gloomy glance.

"Frankie," said Tommy, "it's for five hundred dollars. And where's the target that you're going to miss? Where's the target, Mr. Grant?"

"Well, Jack?" Harry Grant smiled.

"Why—the fence post—that'll do."

"Very well," said Mr. Grant. "But we want a smaller target than that."

Still speaking, he stepped before them, and it seemed that his head was turned across his shoulder toward them, when a revolver slipped into his hand and exploded.

"Now," said he, stepping back, "I want to see one of you put a notch in the new hole that's in that post, yonder!"

Frank, with an exclamation, raced forward and examined the post. He turned with a shout of awe:

"Clean in the center!" he cried.

They could all see it—a little hole.

Frank and Tommy stood side by side at a line and steadied

their revolvers in their hands, while they watched the post
grimly and each other with sharp side glances. It was not hard
to see that these two brothers did not waste love upon one
another.

"Where did you learn that?" asked Jack Mayo of Grant.

"I never forgot it. I knew it in the old days, man. And I
practice enough to keep my hand in."

"Even in New York?"

"Even in New York!"

But there was a shadow of doubt, for the first time, in the
face of Jack Mayo.

"Are you ready?" asked Frank Mayo.

"I'm ready, Frank."

"You can't rattle me," said Frank. "You can't throw me
off my stride. Blaze away."

"Show me the way," said Tommy. "You're the oldest, I
guess."

"Lead off, Frank," called his father. "Why are you waiting?"

"Speed—*and* accuracy!" said Harry Grant. "Hit that post
and hit it quick, and speed counts as much as straight
shooting!"

He stood beside them. "When I clap my hand!"

It was an admirable draw that Frank Mayo made. His gun
whipped out like the end of a lash as it is cracked, and it
exploded at the hip.

"Miss!" said Grant instantly, without an apparent glance at
the post. "Tommy, now!"

His hands struck together, and the revolver of Tommy sped
into his hand full as fast as Frank's had done—or was it just a
hairbreadth faster? Just that shade of increased speed which
makes all the difference between living and dying, at times?

His gun exploded, and the little hole in the center of the
post widened a significant trifle.

Harry Grant did not speak. He remained for a moment,
staring at the boy, as though what he had seen in the face of
the latter at the instant of shooting was worth much reflection,
much steady thought. Jack Mayo had rushed to the fence post

and now he turned and came striding back with a frown on his face.

"Tommy got in a plumb lucky hit," he said. "But the next whirl is where luck don't count so much. Rifles, now! Rifles and Frank go together. Dead cool and certain!"

He stepped back. "Speed ain't what you want now," went on Jack Mayo. "Not speed—but certainty, eh? And that's where Frank is dead sure!"

He waved toward the post.

"Trim that hole out bigger, Frank!"

"That?" said Harry Grant with scorn. "That for a target? No, sir, but what about the hawk, up yonder?"

They looked and saw the hawk whirling swiftly, effortlessly through broad circles against the clear blue of the sky.

"Try it," said Frank to his brother, his teeth clenched with rage and determination.

"There wouldn't be a target for you to hit," said Tommy. "There'd be nothing but an empty sky after I shot. Take your turn, Frankie!"

Frank favored his brother with a poisonous glance and then, dropping to one knee, he raised the gun and with the muzzle followed the flight of the hawk for an instant. The gun spoke—and surely it would have been a dead hawk, had it not been for a slight variance in the wind—or perhaps it was a freak of fancy that made the hawk push back against the air with a sudden flirt of its strong wings. At any rate, there was only a flirt of feathers knocked from it—little feathers that shone transparent in the sunlight as they fluttered slowly down toward the earth.

Frank groaned, watching his last chance float away from him. However, if he had lost, surely his younger brother had lost also. He had squatted cross-legged on the ground, with his own rifle carried loosely and carelessly before him.

"Watch, Frankie," said he, while the hawk, recovering its momentum with swift wing beats, shot away into the sky; "watch and learn. It's not a hawk, but five hundred dollars

that you're shooting at. It's not five hundred dollars, but
Porter's Hagan, and he's mine!''

With the last word, which was a shout of joy, he sprang to
his feet, and at the same moment brought the rifle butt solidly
into the hollow of his shoulder. The gun spoke—and the
hawk sagged downward from the blue, tumbled past the line
of the trees, and thudded lifeless on the ground.

5

It was not Frank Mayo who seemed most affected by surprise and disappointment; it was the father, who stared from one son to the other in a bewildered fashion. At length he burst into a fluent cursing and started toward the house, with a muttered word thrown over his shoulder to the effect that he would return in a short time to be with them. Frank followed at once. He made no pretense of good will to his brother but turned upon his heel and stalked gloomily away.

These things were carefully observed by Harry Grant, though no comment upon them was visible in his facial expression. When he turned from the other two as they disappeared, he saw Tommy sitting on a rustic bench, or rather lolling in an attitude of as much ease as possible, his hands folded behind his head, his gaze wandering through the branches of the tree above him toward the sky beyond.

"What are you thinking of?" asked Grant. "Porter's Hagan?"

"No, of you," said the boy.

Harry Grant started a little. "And what of me?"

"Why was it worth five hundred to you?"

"I put that on your father. He lost a little bet to me."

"It wasn't only favoring Frank, then," observed Tommy with a lazy smile. "It was money, too? Well, but you put up five hundred on *my* chance."

"I did," said Harry Grant.

"Tell me why."

"You killed Conrad Black."

"Aw, that was luck."

"Son," said the older man, "I used to know Conrad Black. And it wasn't luck!"

The lax body of the boy gathered, and he sat up and stared. Not a word was said, but his brown eyes were searching Harry Grant's mind, as that mind had not been searched in many a day.

"You're not a fool," said Tommy, and grinned.

"Is that what you were thinking about me?"

"I was wondering how you could be a friend of dad's— and shoot the way you do?"

"Why?"

"Dad can shoot pretty fast and pretty straight. But his style is all off. You shoot the right way—the same way that I do."

There was enough calm egotism in this remark to balance against any compliment paid to Mr. Grant. The latter coughed behind his hand.

"Where did *you* learn to shoot, young man?" said he.

"By watching," said Tommy, and yawned.

"Watching who?"

"Dad and Frank. Seeing the things they did that was wrong."

"Tell me a few of them."

"Acting as though a gun wasn't a piece of 'em. Acting as though a gun wasn't a friend. You got to trust a gun, or a gun won't trust you. Isn't that right?"

"I suppose so. What about riding my mare and what about making her show off?"

Well, I've got to act like a fool most of the time around dad, or he'd have me at work—or turn me out. So, most of the time, I fall off when a horse turns loose and bucks. Usually, I can make a horse buck without dad seeing me. And I don't mind falling off. There's a way of doing it without getting hurt so bad. You land across your shoulders, you know. Looks as if you'd hit on your head!''

Harry Grant grinned. "Tommy, will you tell me why you care to live like this—doing nothing—making nothing out of yourself?''

"Just resting,'' said Tommy, "and getting ready for the big time coming. And it starts today!''

"What!''

"Me and Hagan.''

"You start?''

"We do.''

"For what?''

"Up or down—I don't care what way. The first place where there's a good time waiting.''

Mr. Grant rubbed his chin. He stared at Tommy with eyes made mild with thought. "Here comes your father,'' he said. "Take that money and go get Hagan—and come back here. Do you understand?''

"Here? I should say not!''

"Don't you think,'' asked Grant, "that I might be able to lead you to a good time?''

Upon this suggestion Tommy pondered only for a moment, and then he nodded gravely.

"I see now,'' said he. "You came here for me. You came here for the man that beat Con Black!''

"Tell me one thing,'' replied the other indirectly. "How much have you practiced with a gun?''

"Oh, they've seen me when I practiced.''

"And missed?''

"*They* thought that I was missing. If we aimed at a tree, Frank and me, he'd hit the trunk. And I'd miss it—and only trim off a twig!''

He chuckled and nodded. "That's the way I've been missing. But Frank—he was born to miss anything worth hitting! He couldn't have hit five hundred dollars if he were three feet away from it!"

All of this seemed so much to the taste of Mr. Grant, that when the boy had ceased speaking, he waited only for the return of Jack Mayo and the payment of the debt. And that debt was paid with a groan.

"I'll have to face Mary, after this. Oh, Harry, what a lucky devil you are! The one day that Tommy woke up, you had to be around to make money by it! Born lucky!"

Harry Grant merely smiled; then he accompanied Tommy up the hill and beyond to the Porter place. Tommy sat a bald-faced roan, with a stumbling gait, sitting loosely in the saddle—not always facing the front. Sometimes he slumped over with only one leg across the saddle, while he stared at a bluejay above—above some stealing, creeping beast among the trees, and striving to get shelter from the eyes of men.

Once he turned clear around in the saddle, hooking his knee over the back of the saddle while he watched something behind him. And, while in that position, he caught by heel and finger tip and slumped down until his trailing hand caught up a piece of shining quartz which attracted his attention.

Harry Grant was delighted and amazed. There were so many contrasts in this fellow—so many odds and ends of queerness that Grant could not make out whether he were a man or a child. He even began to suspect that the loose, sleek body of this fellow might be as strong as it was soft—like the muscles of a cat, supple as silk and tough as iron.

They did not talk a great deal. Grant was content in watching his companion, and his companion was content to watch the scene around him. Not that he was alert and alive. No, his restlessness was like that of a child which cannot remain very long in one position without falling asleep. As he turned his head here and there and looked up and down, his eye remained dull, always—not always, perhaps. But the interest which appeared in it was not longer lived than a spark.

So they journeyed to Porter's, finding Mr. Porter in his backyard, storming at a hired man who was not turning the grindstone to suit the fancy of Mr. Porter, who was bearing down on the wet, whirling stone with an ax that cut the water from the surface. He glanced sidewise at his visitors; and, if he appeared interested in the appearance of Mr. Grant, his interest went out like a snuffed light when he looked at his neighbor's son.

He merely grunted at Tommy, although he gave a cheerful greeting to Harry Grant.

"I hear that the price of Hagan has dropped," said Tommy, by way of "how do you do?"

"Since when have you heard it?" asked Mr. Porter with another scornful grunt.

"Down, but still too high," said Tommy. "I hear that you're asking three hundred and fifty dollars for him!"

"Three hundred and—say, young feller, have you come up here to waste my time? Stranger, might it be that young Mayo has guided you up here on business with me?"

"My name is Grant," said the other. "I've merely come along because I believe that Tommy wants to buy your horse—at a reasonable figure."

"*Him* buy my hoss!" snarled Mr. Porter. "That shamble-shanked good for nothin' buy my Hagan? Mr. Grant, it's plain that you ain't seen my hoss or you wouldn't of listened to no such nonsense from Tommy."

"What's your price," said Tommy, taking money out of his pocket, "if I can ride him?"

"Ride him? I ain't going to be bothered paying no under-taker's bill for you, Tommy. Not me!"

Tommy was shuffling the money bill by bill and counting it aloud: "Eighty—one hundred—one twenty—one forty-five—"

"Is that real money?" yelled Porter.

"Look at a handful of it," said Tommy with a sleepy smile. "You might own part of that money if you were to give up Hagan for it."

Mr. Porter looked blankly at the young man. "By jiminy," said he, the mildness of the oath proving the depth of his emotion, "I think that you mean business!"

"I do."

"Come along, then, and get yourself killed. It'll be a small loss to the world."

6

"But why a nine-foot fence?" asked Grant, when he came, at last, before the enclosure which held the famous horse. "I've never heard of a horse that could wriggle over much more than seven feet."

"Hagan ain't a hoss," said Porter. "He's part devil, part grizzly bear, and part eagle. I had him behind an eight-foot fence. He got his forelegs over when he jumped and that was enough for him. The rest of him followed. First thing I knew, he was on the ground."

"And away?"

"He was too lamed to run very far. We got him back. It took a dozen of us. He only had three legs, but he fought like three devils!"

"Well," said Grant, "it sounds odd. But this fence is really a palisade. Made of whole tree trunks. Did you have to do that?"

"Partly he's quick and mean; partly he's patient and mean," said Mr. Porter. "Put him in a corral and, if he can see his way out, he'll *get* himself out. So we had to put him behind a solid wall. We tried planks first. Well, Hagan walked around and sounded that wall with his forefeet. When he got to a place that looked sort of weak to him, he turned around and began to batter it with his heels—you'll understand what that means when you see Hagan! Besides, if he can't kick his way out, he'll chew his way out like a rat!''

They climbed up to the top of a flight of steps built against the fence, and there Grant had his first view of Hagan.

When the three heads of the men appeared above the fence top Hagan appeared to take no notice of them. His head was down, and he seemed to be very busy, working away at his forage—a few random spears of hay which were scattered on the ground of the corral.

Even Mr. Porter did not understand, but Tommy whispered: "It's the bluejay! He's aiming himself at the jay! Now keep quiet and watch him work!"

For one of those most mischievous thieves and worthless vandals in the bird world had lighted on the ground, within the corral, and was busily examining the intricacies of a pine cone which had fallen from an overhanging tree. With beak and claw and brilliant flirting wings, the jay probed the nooks and the crannies of the rolling cone. In the meantime, Hagan drifted nearer.

His manner was most casual. His ears were not flattened. He even switched his tail occasionally, flicking the end of it over the black satin of his flank where a fly had rested. Now and then, he stamped a little, as a horse will do when other flies have settled on its belly and cannot be reached.

At these stamps, the jay sometimes whirled and lifted a wing stroke or two in the air. But it instantly settled down when it saw that Hagan was merely working busily at the straws of hay—only incidentally coming nearer to him at every step.

Then—when the jay's back was turned—came the final rush—horrible and sudden and quick as a tiger's leap. As the jay rose with a frightened scream, Hagan reared and struck down the lovely bird with a hammer stroke. An instant later there was only a vague, crimson blur, beaten well into the ground of the corral.

And now Hagan was willing to pay some attention to his human visitors. He turned about and lifted his beautiful head to regard them. How gentle and intimate he seemed, and how soft was his eye; as he cocked his head to the side, he seemed like a favorite pony, a child's pet, expectant of an apple, or a bit of sugar.

But when he stepped lightly toward them, two of the watchers drew back. It was not enough that they were nine feet from the ground. They shrank, as they would have shrunk from a charming devil. Seeing them draw back, Hagan turned his back on them and returned to sniff at the dark blot of moisture at the edge of his corral.

"Nice, ain't he?" asked Porter through his teeth.

Mr. Grant did not answer. It was a mighty horror—but the horror was linked with something else which made his heart struggle and rise. He knew horses, did Harry Grant, and he had paid for that knowledge, as a man is apt to do—with many a year of careful study and attention, and with tens of thousands lost, because his knowledge had been just a fraction of a second poorer than he thought it was.

One never graduates from the school of horses, but still one's standard grows, and little by little there is born in the mind—for it can never exist, in fact—something very near to the perfect horse, with speed and supple strength and lithe, marvelous beauty. Mr. Grant had such an ideal tucked away in his mind, of course.

That was why he stared at Hagan and rubbed his eyes and looked again. Sometimes he watched where the sun flashed, as from metal, from the sleekly polished shoulder—sometimes he looked to the round, black feet. Suddenly he touched the shoulder of Mr. Porter. "What price?" he whispered.

Mr. Porter turned his head and looked at him with sympathy, but with amusement also. "I know, it gets folks that way, the first time they see him. But the blue jay wasn't an accident. He's killed two men, partner. Two fine, hard-riding men, I can tell you. And I stood by and watched him work!"

"I've done my share of riding," said Harry Grant, pulling

his belt a notch snugger and moistening his dry lips, while his glance still hung on the horse. "And a man can't live— forever!"

"Try him," said Mr. Porter, "and your life will end right here and now. But, if you want to, step right up and take your turn. It's Hagan against the world, so far as I'm concerned!"

However, there was something, not of kindness, but of ringing cruelty in his voice. It made Mr. Grant turn his head sharply from the stallion and look at the man.

"As bad as that, is he?"

"I've rode in my *own* day," said Porter. "But I never clapped eyes on anything like him. Never! So don't be a fool."

"He's not so big," said Grant. "He's not fifteen three—"

"He's two inches more than that."

"Impossible!"

"I've had the standard on him. He looks smaller. That's because he's made right. A thing that's made right, it sort of tucks away easy into a man's head!"

"I know." Grant sighed. "But, ah, what a horse!"

"Yes," said Porter, "that's what everyone has said in turn around these parts of the country. Oh, he's a pretty good picture. But you can't ride a picture, can you?"

"There *does* seem to be a devil in him." Mr. Grant sighed. "So he can be used for nothing but breeding?"

"Him?" said the son of Mayo, twisting his head over his shoulder. "Oh, I suppose that he's good for something more than that! Will you give me a try at him now?"

"Wait a minute," said Grant, drawing his companion back from the fence. Down the steps they walked out of earshot of Tommy.

"This boy," said Grant gravely, "has a pretty poor reputation around here, it seems."

"Aye," Porter grinned. "No reputation at all, I'd say if you asked me."

"Well," said Grant, "I suppose that some people are good for nothing, if they're not good for something strange. I should say that if young Mayo is chewed up and smashed to bits by the stallion, nobody will break their hearts!''

"Not a soul."

"Then why not give him his chance? Because, between you and me, I think that the boy can really ride the horse."

Mr. Porter stared.

"You think that?" he asked.

"I think that. I'll put up a little money on it, if you want to bet."

Mr. Porter made no answer to this proposal. He walked forward with a frown and called to the boy, who leaned over the fence, gazing at the stallion with studious eyes.

"Son," said he, "how d'you propose to gentle Hagan enough to sit on his back? Or maybe you're a fine horseback rider?"

Tommy did not turn his head, but he called: "Aw, I ain't much of a rider, Mr. Porter, but I can hypnotize 'em, you know!"

"You hear that?" growled Porter. "That boy is a born fool."

"Let him try, then," said Grant. "There is no good reason why you should keep a born fool from dying young."

Porter turned his back.

"Then go ahead," said he to Tommy over his shoulder. "Try your hand with Hagan. Here's a witness that I've tried to warn you against it. And you're old enough to of knowed better sense!"

"Three fifty," said the boy.

"Four hundred is the rock-bottom low price for that stallion," said Porter. "You're not going to get me no lower than that. And—hey!"

The last was a yell which was echoed by Mr. Harry Grant also, for as Mr. Porter spoke, it seemed that young Mayo lost his balance. He toppled, sprawling, over the top edge of the fence and disappeared, floundering into the corral beneath.

Mr. Grant and Porter exchanged glances of expectant horror. But they heard nothing. There was no sudden rush of hoofs. There was no battering of the stallion's feet; there was no scream of agony from young Mayo.

Instead, there was a deep silence—or was that the murmuring of a human voice from within the corral? Yes! Now the latch of the door within the corral was stirred with a groan; the door swung open, and Hagan walked forth into the free sunshine and the air—with nothing to restrain him from breaking away into the wilderness except the hand of Tommy Mayo, laid lightly upon his neck!

7

Instantly Mr. Porter leaped for the nearest tree and, placing himself behind the trunk, he called out: "Hey, you young fool! Hey, Grant, get out your gun—and if he rushes, shoot to kill! I ain't got a gun!"

That was a wail—that last phrase. One would have thought that the stallion would have this man in his mind and would embrace this opportunity to make up for old scores.

And there stood Hagan at the side of Tommy. It was possible for Grant to judge the stallion more accurately, now. For Tommy was a good six feet, and the horse looked big beside him.

"Very well," said Harry Grant. "You have done an extremely clever thing, Tommy. Now I think that you had better put a saddle on Hagan and take him home. It's growing late—and your father may be expecting us!"

He chuckled as he said this. Porter, in the meantime, was looking forth from behind the tree, his eyes great, his face a sickly yellow. But as it began to dawn upon him that the light hand on the neck of Hagan was actually restraining and controlling that great horse, his wonder knew no bounds. Aye, and now the hand fell away. Ah, there went Hagan with the leap of a cat starting away from a dog. Down the hollow he went like a black flash.

Now he was back again in a dazzling circle; and now he was beneath once more, flirting his heels in the air, stamping and snorting, and then neighing with a wild delight at his freedom. He plunged into the air in full gallop, caught at the head of a little sapling, tore it away, and rushed on again.

"He's gone!" Porter groaned, standing with his hands clasped before him very much like an awe-stricken child. "He's gone and he'll never be taken again. There ain't no human brains in the world that will ever be able to handle him, after what he's learned with me! The smell of a man will mean as much to him as ever it meant to any wolf. Oh, Tommy, you've done a fine thing for yourself and for the breed of horses in these here mountains! He's gone! Hagan is gone!"

As a man might have stood and bewailed the departure from his life of all the beauty that had ever come into it, so Porter stood with a stricken face.

Grant looked askance at him, as though surprised to find so much emotion in him. Then he turned his attention to the boy. Tommy displayed not the slightest emotion; he was busily counting out the money. Four hundred dollars in crisp twenty-dollar bills passed into the hands of Mr. Porter; he took them as though he were accepting a penny.

Hagan was gone! And here was a young fool, trying to whistle back the wind! Here was Tommy Mayo whistling to the great black to return! It was only chance, of course, that made the horse turn and race up the slope from the hollow; only chance that made him head straight for Tommy. Perhaps it was a dangerous charge, for he came like a thunderbolt, his ears flattened, his tail streaming straight out behind him by the speed of his going.

He checked himself in the last instant by a pair of stiff-legged bounds and whirling around, flung his heels in the general direction of Porter, then came to a halt with his head not an inch from the shoulder of his new master.

There was no doubt about it. Tommy had established the most perfect control over the fine horse. Mr. Porter looked on with all the astonishment of one who has seen a city fall, or a miracle.

Harry Grant could not help taking pity on Porter and explaining. "It's not so much as you think. Just remember that Tommy, unknown to you, has been sneaking away from his father's house at night and coming up here. He's been working for years at the taming of the stallion."

Porter merely shook his head. "There ain't no way of explaining that," said he. "If you spent a million hours talking to a mountain, would the mountain understand? No more could any human being talk the sort of a language that that hoss would understand! Nothing but the devil would be able to say the sort of words that he would know. Is this flabby kid—this here Tommy Mayo—is he the sort of a devil that can talk to Hagan?"

"Look!" said Grant, by way of answer.

Yonder was the tall stallion, stepping with grace at the side of the youth as they went up the path toward the house.

"I dunno," said poor Porter. "But it ain't right. It ain't right. There's something that ain't natural about it!"

It was mysterious, indeed—and beautiful, and very strange, in the eyes of Grant.

He said, at last: "There's no telling. One can't make out some things. And when one comes face to face with a mystery, the best thing to do is to enjoy it and to ask no questions, whatever!"

"Will you change saddles?" asked Grant.

Tommy turned back on him. He seemed to stand taller; to be more lithe and manly, at the side of the stallion.

"A saddle like that on a horse like Hagan?" said he. "Not for me, Mr. Grant! I've seen the right sort of a saddle for him. I'll wait until I get it."

"A saddle like this one of mine, then?" asked Grant, curious.

"No," said the boy. "When I ride I don't want to work. I want to rest."

He mounted the saddle on the bald-faced roan and in another moment Grant and he were turning back toward the house of Jack Mayo. Hagan roamed through the woods about them or frolicked before them down the road. But at Tommy's whistle, he came back to the side of his master.

There was no temptation in the mind of Grant to ask questions. He remembered how his own mare, Dolly, had obeyed the will of that young rider the first time that he sat on her back. That was enough to convince him that all the ways of this boy were not to be understood by a common mortal. It was only wonderful to him that Tommy Mayo could have lived so long, without giving some hint of himself to those who were around him.

He knew, too, that he had come to the thing that he wanted. His quest was ended. A new work was prepared for him. It was one thing to have found the man he needed; it was still quite another before he should have attached Tommy firmly to him. However, there should be time for that. In the meantime, he would rest and turn the matter over in his mind. Surely there would be no need for him to pass on hurriedly from the house of Jack Mayo!

Harry Grant, thinking in this wise, heaved a great breath, and the set features of his face relaxed a trifle. After that, there was little time for him to think. They had swung onto the road, and a party of half a dozen cowpunchers sighted them and sighted Hagan.

There was a yell and then a chorus of whoops. They put the spur to their horses and surrounded Grant and his companion. But here was Hagan taking refuge at the side of his master, dancing with ears flattened, head raised, and eyes filled with the devil indeed.

There was a chorus of wild enthusiasm and of wild questions. Why was Hagan there? Why was he not running madly away across the hills? How did it happen that Tommy Mayo, of all the men in the world, was the one who had accomplished this feat? Those cowpunchers followed the two in a close escort as far as the Mayo place; there one admiring group was replaced by another, for Jack Mayo and his eldest son, Frank, and his good wife, Mary, had to come out and exclaim.

Only Frank stood in the background, struck dumb with envy. He had gone through all of his life without the slightest challenge to his supremacy from his younger brother. Now he found the fruit of all of his industry and the long years of patient labor apt to be outclassed by one wild day in the life of lazy Tommy! Surely the gods were unjust!

But where could the great stallion be kept? They held a conference on this point and could not reach any conclusion, whatever, until the point was brought up to the actual master of the horse. He merely laughed.

"I'll let him run loose the same as he is now. He'll take care of himself."

"Let him run loose!" shouted Mary Mayo. "Let him run loose? Let five hundred dollars' worth of horseflesh run loose?"

"Four hundred dollars, mother," corrected Tommy, yawning.

"Five hundred or five thousand," she insisted, "now that there's someone that can ride him!"

"Thanks," said Tommy.

"I only hope," said she gloomily, "that you don't ride him to the devil! But would you leave him out here, Tommy, all the night?"

"Why not?"

She threw her hands above her head. "Will you listen to him? Do you want him stolen?"

"Who'll put a rope on that horse?" he asked.

Frank Mayo made a sudden gesture with his hand, and though the stallion had his back turned and was snuffing at a border of flowers beside the roadway, he leaped instantly, standing there winged, as it were, ready to swoop off in any direction—or perhaps to charge straight home! One could not tell from the eye of the black horse what stirred in his mind.

"But he'll run off!" growled the father.

"He'll stay pretty close to where I am," said Tommy with the calmest assurance. "You'll find that when the morning comes he won't be any farther away than my voice will carry."

"He's sure of himself," said Mary. "Every fool is sure of himself until he finds out his folly, and then he's the last one to find it out!"

Tommy, turning his back upon the argument, walked slowly toward the house, lounged through the doorway, and disappeared. The rest stared with awe after him, as though the door, through which he had disappeared, might be able to speak to them in explanation of this mystery.

"Was he hypnotizing that hoss?" asked Jack Mayo at last.

"You've seen as much as I've seen," said Harry Grant. "If I knew what did it, I'd be trying the same thing myself."

"Porter's Hagan!" Frank Mayo sighed. "Who'd of thought that Tommy could ever handle that devil of a hoss!"

"Never you mind, Frank," said Mary Mayo. "If you want a fine, upstanding hoss, I'll see that you get one!"

"Aye," murmured poor Frank. "But it's not the money. It's the getting with one's own hands! And he got Hagan that way!"

8

When the dinner was over that night, Harry Grant decided that there was nothing for him to gain by remaining downstairs with the rest of the company. What he wanted was a chance for long conversation with Tommy, and there seemed no possibility of that.

Besides, Mary Mayo was monopolizing the conversation with her plans for the future of the famous stallion. She was suggesting ways in which Tommy could campaign with the horse. For instance, down in Texas there were those quarter-mile races where the cowpunchers would bet everything they owned—to their very saddles and bridles—on the outcome to back their favorites. Much would be gathered by the black horse in a tour of that district. And she was eager to have Tommy enter upon the fruitful campaign.

"But he'll be gone by the time that the morning comes! Go to the window and call him, Tommy!"

But Tommy was found to be fast asleep in his chair!

Grant excused himself with the plea of the greatest weariness. Travel had exhausted him that day, he declared, and so they showed him to his room. The moment he was alone in it, he began certain preparations which would have amused and entertained the rest of the household greatly, if they could have seen him. First, he examined the door of the room, making sure that it was strongly hinged and of new, good wood. He looked to the lock, to which there was no key.

This, however, did not inconvenience him very greatly, for he presently produced a bunch of keys of many shapes and sizes from his pockets. He gave these a shake that made them open up in his hand like a flower of many petals, under the sun. He did not have to try many keys. One might have thought that he had been the maker of that lock and that he understood all about it. The very first key that he used, fitted the lock to perfection and turned the stout bolt into its socket.

Having made sure that the door was first fast behind him, he continued his observations, going, first of all, to the closet. This he examined in every nook and cranny with a little pocket electric torch which he carried with him. Having made certain that the walls of that closet were strong and secure, he went to the window.

This was a matter which gave him far greater concern, for the window was close under the eaves of the house, at this point. He leaned out of the window, looking up and down. Both ways seemed unsatisfactory to Harry Grant.

After a moment, he discarded coat, vest, and shoes. Slipping onto the windowsill, he balanced himself there with caution and agility, trying the strength of the gutter at arm's length above that window. The gutter was very strong and metal sheathed on the inside.

Mr. Grant, without further hesitation, fastened both hands upon the edge of the eaves and swung himself up to the roof with remarkable skill. The instant that he came over the edge of the gutter, he flattened himself and lay there, waiting and watching. Nothing stirred but the wind through a big tree on the farther side of the house.

He stole in his stockinged feet to the top of the roof and there crouched again to look and to listen. There was nothing of interest to hear or to see. He put his back against the rising brick wall of the central chimney, smoked a cigarette, and raised his face to the stars in the sky above him—dimly blotted, here and there, by wisps of floating cloud.

After this, he returned to the gutter just above his room. The ascent had not been so hard. To reach out was a minor matter; to reach *in* was quite another thing! At least, it would have been to most men. Mr. Grant did not falter for an instant. He merely swung himself down headfirst and hung by his toes from the gutter rim for an instant. Then he caught the windowsill and in another moment dropped on it.

There had not been so much as a whisper made during his exit from the room or during his return to it. But after he was there, he sat down again to consider the ease with which he had gained that room from the roof. He did not like it, apparently; he did not seem to like it at all. After a time, he fixed a pillow in the bed and rumpled the covers, to give, with the aid of the darkness, a fairly accurate representation of a sleeping person in that bed.

For himself, he retired to the farthest corner of the room and lay down to make himself as comfortable as he could. At first, he felt with a blessed sense of relief that he was about to fall asleep, but a little later, his eyes flew open. He was wide awake, listening, thinking once more of the easy reaching distance from the window to the eaves of the roof.

He was wide awake, now. Nothing could keep him asleep from that instant. And he knew it. Another man might have fretted, particularly if, like Harry Grant, one had not slept a great deal in the past month. But Mr. Grant was accustomed to it. He knew, first of all, that the chief strain in insomnia is the *fear* of remaining awake—the *fear* of exhaustion. So he closed his eyes, relaxed himself as much as possible, and there lay through the night.

There were medicines he could take to make him sleep, but he dared not take them; indeed, he dared not sleep more heavily than a wolf sleeps—opening one eye at every stir of the night wind. It was rest of a kind—that sort of rest which kept his face thin and his eyes surrounded with shadows.

When the first gray of the morning began to show across

the window, a feeling of safety came to this refugee, and he dared to rise from the floor and go to his bed. But, as he walked across the floor, it seemed to him that something stirred just outside of the window. He was on his knees, creeping forward on the floor, his body supported by one hand while, with the other, he leveled a gun toward the window. Frightfully tense he waited for another ten seconds. But there was no repetition of the sound.

He gathered his strength and stole softly toward the window, his gun prepared, his jaw set hard. As he stole along, he was fighting ten battles with every step. With every step he was driving himself deeper into an agony. He was at the window at last. In a sort of desperation he forced himself forward and thrust head and gun over the sill!

There was nothing beyond the window, not so much as a sign of a bird nearby. As he was on the verge of heaving a sigh of relief, he saw a figure skulk around a corner of the house. He had only the briefest glimpse of the skulker but he felt that it was the boy, Tommy—not the lax-bodied loiterer of the day before, but one moving with a superb alertness and speed and strength—Tommy!

He felt at first like laughing with his relief, but he began to frown, instead. What did Tommy mean by daring to steal up and spy upon him? Or had Tommy, indeed, dared to climb up the side of the house to gain the window of his father's guest and so look in upon him? Had he, in this very instant during which that guest roused himself and stood up, retreated down the face of the house again? It did not seem quite humanly possible.

Yet, as he looked down the sheer side of the house, he could see that a very clever climber—a veritable sailor—might be able to clamber up the wall, moving from one window to the next above, and helping himself up the drainage pipe.

Then he saw where the dust had been wiped away from the edges of the boards!

Mr. Harry Grant began to curse with a heavy earnestness.

Tommy had chosen to risk his neck for a mere glance at the sleeping guest. What would Tommy have thought when he found that this guest was sleeping on the floor with a dummy arrangement in the bed?

Mr. Grant did not like it. Also, he had a great desire to break the neck of Tommy. But he lay down in this early dawn light. For some reason, after the coming of Tommy, he felt as though he were secure against all outside attack. All that he did was to unlock the door of his room. Then sinking upon his bed, he was instantly lost in a deep sleep.

He slept until the breakfast hour, slept through the tap which Frank Mayo made at his door, slept until Jack Mayo pushed open the door of the room and looked in. Indeed, he slept, while that door was being opened; but before it was actually wide and the head of Mayo had appeared, Mr. Grant stirred with a frown of agony; then he sat up, drew a gun, and leveled it at the gradually yawning door.

However, Mr. Mayo knew something of yore about the habits of the guest who was in his house that morning. Without showing his head, he first said quite softly: "It's only me, Harry."

"Only you!" said Grant. "Well, come in!"

Jack Mayo stood in the door. "A sound sleeper, Harry, I see."

"Always a good sleeper. A good quiet house that you have here—and I haven't opened my eyes all night long!"

He was down at the breakfast table a little later, making his apologies to Mary Mayo. But his apologies were not wanted, because there was a far more interesting topic of conversation.

Outside the window there could be seen the glorious form of the stallion standing on the hillside, cropping the grass where it was sweetest on the lawn under the shade of the big trees in the park. All eyes were turned toward him. All thoughts were centered upon him—all except the thoughts of Mr. Grant.

For he, as he ate his breakfast, was meditating upon the fact that if the enemy he feared on that night had been

Tommy Mayo, he could never have lived to see more than the first gray of the morning light. And at the same time a bullet would have torn its way through his heart.

The thought made Mr. Grant a little pale. And he said to himself: "It's the last time that I sleep inside of a house, if I can help it!"

9

There was a ride through the valley after breakfast, not with Jack Mayo alone, but with Mary, who was far more able to explain what had already been done in the building up of the farm. She showed Harry Grant the places which she hoped to terrace, one day, and she estimated deftly in each case the increased income which would result.

By the time that the party returned to the house, there was no doubt left in the mind of Mr. Grant. His old friend was well on the way to becoming a millionaire. However, it was not money that meant much to Mr. Grant at this time. It was something far more valuable than the cash plunder which he had seen in his mind's eye, the moment that he caught sight of the rich farm in the valley. What he saw was life itself!

He expected that the execution of his plan would take a long time, and so he had made himself very agreeable during that morning ride, managing to make Mary Mayo invite him to spend a month with them—a cordial invitation which he had cordially refused.

A week would either make or break him in this case, as he was well aware. With a young man, one wins early or not at all. What he wanted to put in his wallet, in short, was not money, but the qualities which he saw in the son of his host.

Mary began to worry before the party had returned to the house, for as they passed a nearby field, she pointed out a plowing land incompleted, with no plow team at work upon it.

"Is Frank sick?" she suggested to her husband.

"He doesn't know such a thing as sickness," said Jack Mayo. "But he's sort of blue and downhearted since his brother beat him out of the five hundred dollars."

"By some low trick!" said Mrs. Mayo bitterly.

"But after all, it was good shooting. I've rarely seen better!" said Harry Grant.

This compliment was received by the father in utter silence. At this Grant wondered; for it is an odd thing, indeed, to find a man who cannot take pride in his son.

"You're not fond of Tommy?"

"How can I be fond of him," said Jack Mayo, "when I can't understand him, and he can't understand me?"

That was the explanation. It pleased Grant more than anything else which had been said during the ride.

When they came to the house he put up his horse and then went, without his host or his hostess, for a walk in the parked circle in front of the ranch house. On the farther side of a huge tree he found what he wanted: Tommy and Frank Mayo sitting side by side. Tommy had finished writing on a piece of paper and he looked up to Grant with a smile, whereas Frank Mayo looked up with a start and a frown, and then colored hastily.

"You're in the right time!" said Tommy. "You can be our witness."

He extended the paper.

"No, no!" cried Frank, turning redder than ever.

He tried to interpose, but the sheet was already in the hand of Harry Grant, who asked: "Do you wish me to read this?"

"I want you to sign it," said Tommy, "as a witness. You object, Frank?"

"It has to be somebody," said Frank sullenly. "Mind you, Mr. Grant, this is no job of my seeking. This is all Tommy's idea."

Mr. Grant, reading the paper, whistled softly. "I think that I'd better read this aloud," he said.

"Fire away!"

He read accordingly:

"I, Tommy Mayo, being in my right mind and the full possession of health and all of my senses—"

Tommy broke in: "I thought that that would sound sort of extra legal, you know!"

"I know," said Grant. "It sounds solemn enough. I think that solemnity counts a good deal with a jury."

He continued his reading:

"—do hereby convey, assign, and transfer to my brother, Frank Mayo, for the sum of twelve hundred and fifty dollars, to be hereafter paid to me, all of the share of the estate of my father, Jack Mayo, that may be willed to me by him or that may become my property in any way other than through the death and the proved will of my brother Frank Mayo."

The signature of Tommy was at the bottom of the sheet.

"You are giving up your half of what ought to be about a cool million, Tommy," announced Mr. Grant.

"If I hang onto the half of the million, I'll be an old man before I get it. Dad won't last forever. But Mary will hang on till the halls fall down. I'd rather have a fair start and a good horse under me and take my chances as I find 'em!"

"Very well!" said Grant.

What he heard was music to his ear.

"I've tried to argue him out of it," said Frank Mayo, looking down at the ground. "But it looks as though we're not good enough to suit Tommy here at home—not since he's got the new hoss!"

"Look!" said Tommy, whistling softly.

The black stallion glided out from the trees fifty yards away, looked at his new-found master, and welcomed him with a little softening of the eyes and pricking of the ears. Not even a dog could have been more eloquent.

"Well," said his brother, "it seems to make a whole lot of difference to Tommy. When he insisted—well, I suppose that he'd go away, anyhow, and never come back."

"I suppose that you've thought of all of those things," said Grant calmly. "But for my part, it makes not the slightest bit of difference. Tommy is old enough to know his own mind, and if he insists upon doing this foolish thing, he must be allowed to have his own way. Must he not?"

"I suppose so!" said Frank, now able to lift his head again.

Harry Grant suddenly wrote: "Witnessed on this day, with a full knowledge of the facts in this paper, by Harry Grant."

He handed the paper back to Frank.

"No!" broke in Tommy sharply. "I'll have that paper— until I get the cash. Hand over the cash, Frank, and then you can have it!"

By some mysterious sleight of hand, he had managed to take the paper from the fingers of his brother. Now he sat back against the tree, grinning at Frank Mayo.

"You don't trust me?" asked Frank with some sadness and some virtuous indignation.

"Not a bit," said the incorrigible Tommy. "I don't trust you an inch. Let me see the coin and then you can have the paper. That's only fair!"

Frank Mayo flushed with anger, yet the game which he was playing was far too great a prize and he could not allow himself to be shunted away by a mere matter of feelings—or for so small an insult as this. He rose and stalked toward the house.

"Well," said Grant, "you're an odd fellow, Tommy."

"Am I?"

He took from his inside coat pocket a little leather case, somewhat like the case in which Mr. Grant kept his fine cigars. When he had opened the case he drew from it the sections of a flute, which he screwed together.

"A musician, too?" asked Grant.

"Sort of a musician in a way, you know."

He tilted back his head until it rested against the trunk of the tree and then, uninvited by Grant, but for his own pleasure, and totally without self-consciousness, he began to blow a crystal shower of notes. They came with such a lightning delicacy that it seemed to Grant almost as though the player were striking bells with the light tips of his fingers—clear, whistling bells that chimed and sang and melted reluctantly from the air. His eyes closed. As he blew, it seemed that he would be smiling for joy of the music, if it had not been that his lips were pursed.

His forehead puckered. Now his eyes opened, and his glance flashed from side to side—like the glance of a wild beast. To Harry Grant, it was as though he had stumbled upon the great god Pan! Neither was he altogether comfortable. He started and stared, almost glad when young Frank Mayo came hurrying back from the house.

However, the arrival of Frank Mayo and his flourish of money was not to interrupt Tommy. He continued to pipe until the song had trilled away to an end.

Then he took the flute, unscrewed it, wiped it with a silk handkerchief, wrapped it again, and restored it gravely to the little leather case. After this, he took out a cigarette and lighted it.

"Well?" he asked Frank Mayo scornfully.

"I've got it all here," said the other nervously. "I suppose that you're going to say that it is all a joke, now!"

"I?" Tommy chuckled. "There is only one joke here—and that joke isn't twelve hundred and fifty dollars. Not a bit of it!"

"Then here you are."

"Never mind counting."

"I'd rather count it all out. I want this to be honest!"

"Oh, you're honest, Frank," said the brother. "You're

honest enough. But I don't want to waste time counting
money! Give it to me!"

"Give me the paper, then!"

"Why, here you are."

The money passed out of one hand; the paper went into
that of the other; and the deed which separated Tommy Mayo
forever from his inheritance was accomplished.

He stood up, brushed the dust from his clothes, and looked
with a smile after Frank Mayo, who with a hunted look and
the paper clutched in both his hands was hurrying off toward
the house.

"Look at him," said Tommy. "Well, he's done for now.
He knows that he's been a crook. And he'll never get over it.
He's poisoned, eh?"

"He's poisoned," admitted Grant, watching the boy like a
hawk. "But why did you do it?"

"Because I thought that Hagan was worth it."

"Hagan?"

"And you."

"And I?" cried Grant, now almost alarmed.

"Of course." Tommy grinned. "I'm not blind. Of course I
know that you've come here fishing for me!"

It was a blow such as Mr. Grant had not received in many a
long year. He considered Tommy with a rather grim look;
then carefully took out and lighted a cigar. As for Tommy, he
merely pushed his hat onto the back of his head and grinned
at his companion.

"Young man," said Grant, "shall I think over that last
remark of yours?"

"I've thought *you* over," said the other, "and I've *looked*
you over, as you know."

"What the devil are you referring to now?"

"Why, you saw me take a peek through your window this
morning while you were lying in the corner on the floor."

"You know that I knew that?"

"Of course. Your face was full of it when you came down
to breakfast."

Mr. Grant turned his cigar slowly in his mouth with lean, bony fingers. He watched and studied the youth.

"You are a little quick for me, Tommy," said he. "I don't know but that you're even a little *too* quick for me."

"Too quick to learn?"

"Learn what?"

"What you know."

"And what's that?"

"How to live sweet and easy and how to do it on no work!"

"No work? The brokerage business is work enough, my young friend."

"Sure," said Tommy, "the *brokerage* business is."

Mr. Grant cleared his throat. "Suppose that we speak frankly with one another," said he. "Let me know exactly what you think of me?"

"I think," said Tommy, "that you could teach me a good many things worth knowing. And I think that you wouldn't think you had a bad bargain."

"What sort of a bargain?"

"Well," said Tommy, "I suppose that I ought to tell you everything that I have in my mind, but I was thinking that you could do a little of the talking yourself! Mr. Grant, you've come here because you need help. You started on this trail because you heard that I downed Conrad Black in a fair fight. You knew that it was a fair fight, no matter what the blockheads all over this part of the country think about it! And you knew that the man who beat Con Black was the man that you needed to get you out of *your* trouble!"

"My trouble?"

"Grant, I don't know who they are, of course, but I do know that they're after you!"

Mr. Grant began to show signs of perspiration. His face flushed. He even had to take out a handkerchief and brush his forehead.

"When you looked through the window," said he, "was I

asleep, although my eyes were open—and was I talking aloud at the same time?''

Tommy shrugged his shoulders. "I'm not a mind reader, if that's what you mean. But a man can't help using his eyes."

"Aye," murmured Grant. "But it seems to me, that you look rather deep. However, go on and tell me the rest of the story!"

"I've about talked myself out. It's your turn."

"I'll talk enough when the time comes. But first tell me about yourself, and why it was that you were willing to sign away half of a million dollars."

"It wasn't half a million," said the boy calmly. "Not at all. If it was the old man alone, I would of got a square deal. But Mary is the one that will settle the will and settle my hash at the same time. And even if she should die before she's a hundred and fifty years old, she's sure to leave a will that will have me ruled out of the game! She'll find some sort of a way to leave nine-tenths of the estate to my brother Frank."

"But even a tenth of a million is a hundred thousand, and most people think that that's worth having!"

"Money for a year or two," said Tommy, yawning. "But not really enough for more than that."

He made a large gesture, as though he were actually throwing away the huge sum of money which he had just mentioned.

"Why not?" asked the other, more and more amazed. "Why not, Tommy? Are you going to spend more than fifty thousand dollars in a year?"

"Me?" Tommy grinned. "Yes, sir, that's exactly what I'm gunna do! I'm gunna spend more than fifty thousand dollars a year. I suppose that you get through with about that much yourself!"

Mr. Grant started again. "Confound you, young man, where have you been finding your dreams?"

"In your face." Tommy grinned again.

"And you find fifty thousand dollars a year there?"

"All the free years, I mean," said Tommy.

Mr. Grant drew back, as one who has heard enough—yes, too much! "I don't follow that idea any too well," he declared.

"Oh, yes you do! You and me, we understand each other pretty well, I guess! I mean, if you want it in plain words, that all the years you're out of prison, you live pretty well. Isn't that so?"

Mr. Grant swallowed hard and then he found it necessary to loosen his collar a little. "Tommy, curse you! I think that you and I will *have* to be friends! Don't you?"

"Sure," said Tommy, "we see through each other too easily. It wouldn't be safe for one of us to have the other floating around loose. That's why we'll have to team it together. Until they get you or until we get them. Who are they, Mr. Grant?"

Mr. Grant drew long and hard on his cigar. "Very well, I'll tell you all that you need to know before long. But in the meantime, I want you to let me understand what is going to get you your fifty-thousand-dollars-a-year spending money?"

"Brains," said the boy, "and hands, and feet."

It was a sufficient answer to make Mr. Grant laugh softly to himself. "Oh, Tommy," said he, "if you're half the man that I think you're going to be, what a great time of it we'll have together."

"Oh," said Tommy, "you haven't seen the half of it!"

"There's still more in the way of tricks that you can show me?"

"Quite a bit. In this line, you know!"

He took out a pack of well-worn cards and shuffled them in the air with the easiest dexterity.

"Right," said the other. "That's the most paying line, of course. Have you really done any work with those cards?"

"Guns," said the boy, "come naturally, I suppose. I *have* to hit what I'm shooting at. But cards are only half natural. I've been preparing for a good many years. Ever since I found out that work and myself didn't get along extra well together!"

Mr. Grant chuckled. "How much?"

"A couple of hours a day," said Tommy seriously. "That's with the cards, you know. Besides that, I've worked up some ways of doing exercises that supple up the fingers. Playing the flute isn't so bad, if you come right down to that. There's some finger work in that!"

"Very true! But let me see if you can deal a hand—even with those worn old cards!"

"I keep the smooth decks for Sundays." Tommy grinned. "What sort of a hand will you see?"

"Poker," said Mr. Grant. "A hand here to my right that will bid up, a hand to me that is better, and a hand to yourself that will cover the pair of us!"

"Certainly," said Tommy. "Though I generally work at a five-handed poker game!"

He shuffled the pack, submitted it to Mr. Grant for a cut, and then he dealt swiftly, the cards flashing in a steady stream from beneath his flying finger tips.

When he had finished Mr. Grant regarded the three nines in the neighboring hand, the full house in his own, and the beautiful set of four jacks which reposed in the dealer's share of the cards!

"A nice deal," said Mr. Harry Grant, "a very nice deal. But, Tommy, I really don't see where I can be of much assistance to you. For you deal about as well as I do—if I have to confess it—and I think that you could make your way pretty well in the world!"

"I could," admitted the other with perfect calm; "I could get along very nicely. But that isn't what I want. I want to start not on the outside, but on the inside. I hate to work, Mr. Grant. I want the melons that are big and juicy, not the dried-up ones that are all rind!"

Mr. Grant extended his hand, and Tommy shook it.

"My dear Tommy," said Harry Grant, "how do you happen to be the son of Jack Mayo?"

"I don't happen to be the son of Jack Mayo," replied the other.

"What?"

"His wife—his first wife—adopted me. That's all that I know about the deal."

"What *are* you, then?"

"If I knew," said Tommy, "would I be here? No, sir, I'd be off, living the life that I was born for—a gentleman's easy life, Mr. Grant!"

"Were you born a gentleman, then?" asked Grant, too interested to be amused by the calm vanity of this youth.

"I think that I may say that I was," said the other, "born to have plenty of money. But since I've been beaten out of that, I'm going to get the equivalent of it out of the world—in hard cash! Do you blame me?"

"My dear boy," said Harry Grant, "only tell me when we are to start on the road!"

"Pronto," said Tommy. "I want to say good-bye to the old man, and I want to roll up my pack. Then we're away."

"With a saddle on Porter's Hagan?"

"Not till we come where there's a saddle worthy of him."

"Tommy, I think that you and I are going to lead a very happy life together."

"Mr. Grant, all I know is, that you're going to lead a *longer* life while you're with me!"

10

Grant might have been expected to have made some response to such whole-hearted confession from the lips of Tommy, but he merely said, in the end:

"I can tell you a pretty long story, one of these days. But all that's worth your knowing now is that you're completely right. Only tell me how you knew that there was more than one after me?"

"By the way you handled your gun," said Tommy instantly, "when you drilled that target in the post for us to shoot at!"

"A whole post to shoot at?"

"A post is smaller than a man, by a good deal! I aimed to figure out by that that it was a gang that was after you. How'll I know any of the boys *in* that gang?"

"I don't know!"

"What?"

"I don't know. I know who's behind them, but what men he'll send to get me, I never can tell. It may be some one-legged cripple begging beside the road. It may be a fourteen-year-old playing with a knife—I expect the steel between my shoulder blades when my back is turned! I never know how it will happen or when it will happen. So I have to keep looking and waiting and watching."

Mr. Grant finished with a sigh which was faintly echoed from the boy.

"I know," said he. "I guessed at the look in your eyes. But while you watch the front, I can watch the back. Is that the scheme?"

"It is."

"And you'll trust me, Grant?"

"As far as you'll trust me, Tommy."

"My hand on that."

"Shake. And the start, Tommy?"

"Now!"

He started toward the house, and Mr. Harry Grant began to walk up and down, up and down, with a light, springing step and a quick turn at the end of his path.

It was a good day, a great day—the greatest day that had come to him in many and many a year. Above all, he promised himself now that he would be able to sleep at night. He knew, without having to inquire, that the sleep of Tommy Mayo would be as light as the sleep of a wild beast, ever in the scent of danger, ever alert, and yet ever calmly relaxed as he, Grant, could never have been. Or they could sit watch and watch about.

Yet there was a shadow in his joy. He had, all his life, gone through the world playing a lone hand. He almost shuddered when he thought of entrusting a full knowledge of his fortunes to another person. Although he shuddered, he knew that there was no other solution. Either freedom with a helper to guard him, or else the prison bars—and hardly safety even there!

Mr. Grant walked and still walked, and the time flowed swiftly beneath and through him, and presently he was roused by the harsh voice of Mary Mayo. Looking up, he found that estimable lady standing just before him on the grass.

She said to him: "You've taken Tommy! Is that it?"

"You're glad, aren't you?"

"Oh, yes," she answered, with amazing calm. "There are some crooks that I can get along with very well. But Tommy doesn't happen to be that sort of a crook."

"He is a crook?" Grant smiled, as though incredulous.

"Oh," said Mary, "I don't think that there's much use trying to pretend with me. Because I think that I understand you pretty well, Mr. Grant. I suppose that you saw everything that was to be seen in Tommy about the first minute that you laid eyes on him. You know that Tommy is crooked. He doesn't *think* straight!"

"Are you sure of that?"

"Yes, sure enough. He isn't the right kind. He's what my father used to call spoiled meat. He ain't got the right sort of insides to make a good man of him."

"Tell me why, if you please?"

Mary smiled upon the other. "Listen, talk right out free and easy with me, Mr. Grant. But don't try to pull no wool over my eyes. Because I don't like it. *You* understand Tommy— and I think that *I* understand you!"

She said this with a certain straightness of expression that made Mr. Grant look down at the ground and clear his throat in some embarrassment.

"My father," said Mary Mayo, "was a pretty hard sort of a man. He brought lots of hard sorts of men into my life when I was just a girl. I learned to know them pretty well, you can be sure. I used to see lots of gunfighters, lots of forgers and safecrackers, lots of all kinds of the boys that have to put a big distance between today and tomorrow if they want to sleep safe. Lots of gamblers, too!"

Grant started back, a little. "I don't understand you!"

"I think you do, though," said she. And she smiled in her odd, mirthless way at him. "I think that you understand a good deal too much for some people—for poor Jack Mayo, for instance. And I suppose that you won't be staying here very long?"

"Do you think that?" said Mr. Harry Grant.

"Yes," said she, "I think that. However, I would like to

have you wait around until my friend, the sheriff, drops in this afternoon. He likes to talk to all of the old-timers. I'm sure that he'd like to talk to you."

"I don't think that he would remember me," said Grant.

"He has a great eye for faces," said she. "And he keeps up with the rogue galleries of several states. He picks up lots of gamblers, as they pass through—the foolish ones that drop off to work this state."

Here she paused again, and Harry Grant suddenly broke into loud laughter. He extended a hand, which she grasped and shook vigorously.

"That's right," said she. "I want to be friendly. But Jack can sign a check for too much money. It makes me sort of nervous to have you too near him."

"If I had intended that," said Grant, "he wouldn't have a penny to his name by this time!"

She shook her head. "Maybe you work as fast as that, but I doubt it. However, when are you taking Tommy away with you?"

"Anytime that you suggest, I suppose."

"Five minutes from now would be better than five hours. Frank Mayo is getting a little restless. He is a stupid boy. But he begins to see that perhaps the part of the ranch which he has just bought out of his savings may not be worth more than twelve hundred and fifty dollars."

"You know about that already?"

"Oh, yes. I have Frank very well trained. That's why Tommy is leaving—because he knows that if he continued to live here a long time, he would have to become as Jack and Frank are. I like to be the captain and the chief engineer all in one, you know!" She smiled sourly on him.

"Tommy is right," said she. "If I were in his boots, I'd rather be a beggar than the son of a rich man who has to act like a hired man. However, if I were in Tommy's boots, I'd figure a bit further than he does. I'd see that crooked living isn't easy living, after all. Because crooked money doesn't stay in one's pocket safely enough. Crooked money has wings. And what's the use of having winged money? I like coin that stays put!''

It was the perfect calmness with which she revealed herself to Grant that amused him. He had expected a great deal of smug hypocrisy. This indifference as to his opinion of her pleased him. It was her tribute to his powers of penetration. She showed him freely a truth which he would soon have found out for himself. Our confessed evil is far less incriminating than the unconfessed which is discovered in us by the inquisitor.

"Tommy and I," said the gambler, "prefer the coins which have the wings, because we like the fun of chasing it.''

She nodded, with her head on one side, and a light in her keen eyes.

"Well," said she, "if I were a man—perhaps—''

"If you were a man," he broke in, "I should have come for you and not for Tommy."

"Yes," said she, coloring a little, "I think that the pair of us would have made a very good living. Good-bye, Mr. Grant.''

She went back to the house. Grant followed a little slowly to get his pack. While he was still in his room, Jack Mayo rushed in on him, full of exclamations.

"We're not going to be gone very long," said Mr. Grant. "Tommy and I are simply going to do a tour of the mountains and come back right away. Tommy wants to train his new horse. And I want to see Tommy work!''

That was enough explanation for that simple soul. As for Frank Mayo, he came and looked askance while he shook hands with Grant. And the latter could not help pouring out his scorn and his anger.

"Frank," said he, "you'll never have happiness. The sort of money that you make will never rest easy with you. The gold that you stack up, will hobble you. It'll be a burden for you to carry, and not a pleasure. You've cursed yourself right at the start by trying to cheat your own brother. And the result is, that he's beaten you in the trade. He's got his freedom—

and some of your money besides! And you've paid a price in order to go on being a slave!''

Frank Mayo winced and left the older man without a word of reply. But the most touching part was between Mary and Tommy. They held hands for a long time.

"I'm almost sorry to be leaving you," said Tommy. "It's been a long fight, but a good one."

"You've made a little winning here," said she through her teeth. "But if you dared to stay here, I should have won in the end."

"The referee was on your side, which wasn't fair."

"Tommy, I'm going to put something in your saddle bag that will be worth more than—powder and lead to you! It's this. Look at it everyday!"

Into his saddle bag, she slipped a small envelope, saying: "I understand everything, Tommy. You want to keep moving all your life. But you have to remember that you can't raise a crop unless you stay to sow where you plow, and reap where you harrow!"

11

At the top of the next hill, they turned and waved back. Tommy was on the back of a common cow pony, with black Hagan ranging far ahead, and Dolly fretting at the halt. Then they dipped over the brow of the hill and went down the farther slope.

"That's that!" Tommy chuckled.

"Never see them again?" asked Grant.

"I'll see the old man, and that's all! But let's forget about them. We've got too much that's worthwhile ahead of us!"

"But, why, Tommy, did you put the price of your heritage and your freedom at exactly twelve hundred and fifty dollars?"

"I'll tell you. A man has to have tools."

"Twelve hundred and fifty dollars' worth of them?"

"I've seen a rifle and a pair of pretty neat revolvers. The three of them will cost me two hundred and fifty dollars."

"What?"

"Well, they're decorated a little. Besides that, I've seen just the saddle and the bridle for the horse. They cost exactly a thousand dollars. That's why I put the price there!"

Mr. Grant did not reply, but he glanced sidewise at this boy again. A thousand dollars for a saddle!

"Clothes, pocket money, and the rest don't count with you?" he asked.

"Not till I get the right kind."

"And if you should turn hungry?"

"I've got salt in my pouch and ammunition for my guns. So I'll never go hungry."

Mr. Grant gave his horse the rein, and they whirled down and through the next hollow at a lively clip. Black Hagan ranged ahead, with a grace like the wind. When his master whooped he would throw up his head and neigh a joyous response. In the meantime, the speed of Dolly began to tell on the honest cow pony which young Tommy rode. Presently the latter was lagging in the rear.

Then, straight behind Mr. Grant, a gun exploded, and a bullet sang past his ear.

Grant jerked his head around, his gun already in his hand. But there he was paralyzed, for the gun had not been fired from an ambush behind him. It was smoking in the hand of Tommy, who was even now putting up his weapon!

"Tommy!" gasped Grant.

"Did you think I was shooting for you?" asked Tommy. "Nope. It was over in the woods, yonder!"

Mr. Grant scanned him with a puzzled air. "What? A squirrel?"

"Does a squirrel have spurs?" asked the boy.

At this, Grant rode through the next screen of saplings and saw, stretched on the ground before him, a tall man lying on his back, with his arms thrown wide, a red hole gaping in his forehead. A dozen paces away, the large, soft eyes of a horse looked through the shrubbery, wondering at the fallen master.

Tommy came through the brush in time to hear Grant say: "O'Neil! They've sent even O'Neil this time! Who next?"

He turned to Tommy with a pale face.

"What did you see?"

"The wind ruffled the leaves a little," said Tommy.

"And I saw the wink of his rifle at shoulder height and the

glint of a spur at his heel. I thought there was no use waiting to ask questions."

Mr. Grant wiped his forehead.

"He would have had me in another minute—another second. He almost had me once before—O'Neil—and now he's turned into this!"

He knelt beside the fallen man and hunted swiftly through his clothes. There were two or three letters, which he opened and read through gravely. But there was nothing else of importance in his wallet. Some fifty odd dollars in cash was taken and pocketed by Mr. Grant. Then he looked to the rifle which lay on the ground near the master. It was a beautiful weapon, beautifully kept. But Mr. Grant passed it on to Tommy.

"Poor old O'Neil!" he said.

He carried the body, with Tommy's help, into the roadway.

"And now the horse?" he suggested to Tommy.

"Not a dead man's horse," said Tommy calmly. "I'll plug along on this one. Leave the horse here to keep O'Neil company!"

A minute or two later, they were on the trail again. It might have seemed strange to some men that Mr. Grant did not make any attempt to thank the man who had saved him from sudden death. But it did not appear to rest heavily upon the mind of Tommy. Instead, he seemed pensive about something else.

Presently, he said: "I'll never reach O'Neil's age."

"What?"

"Oh, no! I'll be burned out long before that. Some take their pleasures slowly and some take them in pills—condensed. I'll take mine condensed, thank you! I'll have my whirl, and there'll be an end to me. Four or five years. That's enough!"

"Four or five years," murmured Mr. Grant, "four or five years! Why, do you plan to be through with the world by the time that you're twenty-six?"

"Of course!"

"While you're still a child?"

"Call it that if you want. But the things I want can't be had for long."

"Such as what?"

"I'll have a bridle alone," said he, "with enough gold on it to make men want to murder me. I'll have a saddle that'll make them want to do *two* murders! I'll have a wallet stuffed until it is almost choked to death."

"How will you get the stuffing for it?"

"Cards, partly. Or now and then I might crack a safe."

"Have you learned how to do that, my talented young friend?"

"You can teach me," said Tommy.

Grant started again.

"*I* teach you? Do you think that I'm a thief?"

The mild brown eye of Tommy was fixed calmly upon him.

"Among other things, you are," said Tommy.

The color which flushed the face of Mr. Grant was not anger.

"You impertinent young rascal!" he exclaimed without heat. "But even supposing that you have a saddle covered with gold, and a horse under the saddle that some men would do a murder for, and a wallet stuffed with stolen money— other people have had as much. Yet they have lived for a considerable length of time!"

He looked at his companion with a significant directness, but Tommy merely grinned.

"You're not a spender," said he. "That's what keeps you safe so long."

Mr. Grant bit his lip. "I've never denied myself a necessity."

"No? Well, I want to begin where you left off. I want friends now."

"Will having friends shorten your life?"

"Yes, because some friend that I trust will kill me in the end."

"Then, you young fool, why do you have them?"

"And live like you—alone—scared of my own shadow? What's that kind of a life good for? No, I'll play my own game and live my own life and keep it pretty full, and when the finish comes, I won't have any regrets."

"What of your sweet life, when your *friends* have betrayed you? You are going to surround yourself with a lot of men who will follow you until they see that they can get more out of you by turning you over to the law? A pretty life, Tommy, but not for me!"

"Three years—four years—five years—I don't know what! But when the finish comes I won't regret it. Only while the fun lasts, I want it to be high—lots of noise—lots of music— and then a bullet to put out the lights. But to grow old and turn lame in the head like my father, or wait until my nerve has rubbed thin—no, I don't want that!"

"Bah!" said Mr. Grant suddenly, "a handsome youngster like you will find a pretty girl, in a year or two, and she'll bowl you over, spill all of this nonsense out of your head, and make you ready to reform and do what she wants you to do. I give you about six months of this freedom of yours before you are tied to an apron string!"

He laughed as though this solution of the problem was a great relief to him. And Tommy laughed, too.

"I wish her luck," said he. "For if ever I find a woman that I love more than I love the life that I intend to lead, confound me, if I know what I'll do!"

"Marry her and reform, of course!"

"I don't think so," said Mr. Tommy Mayo, filled with thought. "I don't think so!"

He said this in such a manner that Grant, starting to make some rejoinder, checked himself and bit his lip again. For the talk had taken a turn which he had not expected. He started out of a black reverie and exclaimed:

"Have you no questions to ask me about the man you killed, and why he was waiting there for me in the shrubbery?"

"Mind you," said Tommy, "what I want out of you is not

news about yourself, because I might find out something that would make *me* want to put a slug through your head!"

"And then?" asked the other, with an ugly intonation.

"And then," said Tommy, "I'd find that I wasn't fast enough with a gun to put you out of the way!"

12

Most men would have considered such a remark about his gun prowess a fine tribute, but Mr. Grant was very far from being a fool, and therefore he considered the remark in silence which lasted until they came to the next halting point in their journey. He was wondering what stranger might find that dead man in the trail behind them, how the news might travel, how the old companions would learn that O'Neil had died on the long trail of Harry Grant, when Tommy stopped his horse.

They were in front of a little shack with a bit of stovepipe sagging crazily above the roof, a more than half-ruined vegetable garden at the side of the tiny house, and a general air of decay and bitterest poverty.

"Why are we stopping here?" Grant asked.

"Because the saddle and bridle are in this house," said Tommy.

"A thousand dollars' worth of saddle and bridle?" exclaimed Mr. Grant. "In *that* shack?"

"Yes." Tommy nodded and swung himself to the ground.

Mr. Grant followed without dismounting and rode close to

the open door of the house until a great brute of a dog rushed out past Tommy and snarled in front of Dolly's knees.

"Steady, boy," said Tommy, and he added to Grant, as the dog's snarl sank to a low, muttering growl: "You'd better stay where you are—and keep in the saddle. This dog has a reputation to keep up, and he doesn't care a bit who he chews up to make it."

There was really no need for Grant to ride any nearer, however, for through the open doorway he could look easily into the interior and see an old man sitting like a cross-legged tailor on a bench, with his spectacles hanging near the tip of his nose and a little board across his knees, on which he was working carefully away at a bit of leather with a knife.

He looked up with nearsighted eyes, that were full of firmness and the knowledge of a craftsman. Perhaps they could hardly look as far as Mr. Grant, but they filled him with the greatest uneasiness and sent a little chill through his heart. For they were the eyes of an honest man, whose life of true creative and honest labor had brought to him nothing but trouble, nothing but poverty. And he, Harry Grant, had invested in the world how many hours of manly, clean-handed effort?

"Ah, it's Tommy again!" said the leather worker.

"It's Tommy," said the boy. "I've come up to look at you and the saddle, again."

"Take it out," said the old man. "Take it out and look it over in the sunlight. There's the saddle hanging from a nail in that sack, over yonder."

Presently Tommy reappeared, carrying the sack and smiling at Grant. Then, out of the bag, he produced a great parcel wrapped about in old rags. When the rags were stripped off there, under the eyes of Mr. Grant was the most dazzlingly beautiful saddle that he had ever seen.

He had been in Mexico where they think nothing of heaping gold and silver upon their horse furnishings. But it was not in the sheer quantity of the gold chasing that the work was remarkable, but the delicacy and intricacy of the

whole design. Harry Grant could not help crying out when he
saw it. He held out his hands instinctively, and Tommy, with
a smile, placed the saddle before him.

It was truly a thing of beauty. The gold lay upon it like fine
highlights—a dainty, brilliant fretting. But the gold and the
gold working was not the chief marvel. Every inch of the
leather was covered with the most intricate design. And what
a carving it was!

"How could a man do it in a lifetime!" murmured Mr.
Grant.

"He didn't," said the boy. "His father started it before
him and just laid out the work—got it started, you might say.
He spent his spare time for ten or twenty years on that there
saddle. And then Will Yeager, yonder, got to work on the
saddle about fifty years ago. He spent odd hours for forty
years on the thing. Ten years ago he finished it."

"And did the gold work, too?"

"No. He was down in Mexico City and got a Mexican gold
worker to put that on."

But the leather carving was the point of importance. There
were rarely any deeply incised figures, but everywhere the
surface was covered with the pattern. Birds, flowers, cactus
of a hundred varieties linked in a border, trees of every sort
that grew in the mountains, animals of prey and those which
were preyed upon—the weasel, the rabbit, the puma, the
deer—all of these things were worked upon that saddle,
closely, yet so grouped that they formed themselves into
dainty designs. Mr. Harry Grant rested his hand upon the
pommel.

It was slightly roughened by the figure of an eagle with
outspread wings, rising fast into the air with a fish in its
talons; halfway down the horn of the saddle was shown the fish
hawk from which the prize had been taken by the pirate—
a torn and dying fish hawk, slain by a stroke of the giant's
beak and now tumbling over and over in its rapid flight
through the air.

That was only a detail. Had all the continent been covered

with a deluge and only this saddle remained, it would have shown, well enough, what the life among the Rockies was like. Every industry was represented; for instance, on the skirt of the saddle, worked as a tiny margin not half an inch wide, there was the prospector who starts out with his hammer in his hand, sighting a course through the mountains between the ears of his high-packed burro.

Here he breaks rock—here he camps for the night—here he breaks rock again. Now he is throwing his hat in the air and dancing! Now a hole opens in the rock face of the mountain; the prospector is toiling luckily within. Last of all, he stands in the center of the barroom floor encircled by admiring friends. His gold belt lies fat and long upon the bar. He is setting them up in honor of the goddess of fortune.

No, it is not the last of the picture, for here is a final picture at the end of the border—a roulette wheel standing by itself. Perhaps it gives a point to all the rest, after all!

Yonder is a more ambitious sketch of a tall, dark forest, with the wood choppers busy in its heart, and a giant pine toppling to its fall. Here is a picture of a swirling corner of the roundup—a flare of dust and a riot of plunging cattle and quick-footed horses with riders in the saddles.

More and more and more! Will you have a picture of an early caravan, like one of those land fleets which used to cruise across the plains and westward in search of gold or empire? Then search the saddle and here it is—yes, here, on the inner flap of the saddle, is a representation of the very thing, from the far-flung outriders who searched for Indians far ahead, to the footsore wanderers who brought up the rear of the procession.

Mr. Harry Grant could not feast his eyes enough on this work of art. "A thousand dollars!" said he. "A thousand dollars!"

He brought his eye closer to the design. "Why," said he, "it is worth looking at through a microscope!"

"A lot of it was *done* under a microscope," he was assured.

"A thousand dollars for this?" said Harry Grant. "Why, the poor old man is mad! You're robbing him, my friend Tommy! He could get ten thousand from a museum for such a piece! A book could be written and filled with pictures out of this one saddle. A thousand dollars! The poor old man has lost his wits! I'd give him five thousand myself!"

"Offer it to him, then," said the boy.

"Do you mean it?" asked Harry Grant.

But he did not wait for a reply. No matter how great the service which he might expect from this young man, the saddle had so charmed him that he seemed very willing to sacrifice the friendship of Tommy for the sake of winning the saddle from him. And now he called to the bent form of Will Yeager:

"Hello! Will Yeager! I've come to take this saddle off your hands!"

The old man, with an exclamation, started up and hurried out from the shack. "You've come for the saddle?" he asked, fitting his spectacles more closely to his eyes.

He scrutinized the stranger with a smile that had a great deal of mischief in it—and mockery, it seemed to Harry Grant, as well.

"A purchase by spot cash and at something above your asking price, if you wish!" And he took out his wallet significantly.

"There ain't more than one price on that saddle," said the ancient. "A thousand dollars is enough. But what kind of a hoss do you aim to buy that saddle for?"

"What kind of a horse?" echoed Grant angrily. "What has that to do with the business?"

"A mighty lot, believe me! A mighty lot! Am I gunna set seventy year of handwork on the back of some ordinary plug of a hoss? It ain't gunna be Will Yeager that does a thing like that! Lemme see what kind of a hoss you would put that saddle on, before you can take it away!"

"As fine a one as you ever have laid eyes on," said Mr. Grant. "You can look her over for yourself."

"That mare you're riding?"

"That very one."

"My eyes get sort of poor and weak, as time runs along," said Mr. Yeager. "I don't know that I can see a hoss, really, as long as there's a saddle and a rider on it!"

Mr. Grant muttered an oath. Yielding with a poor grace to the whim of the old man, he presently sprang to the ground and stripped the saddle from the back of Dolly. Relieved from that binding pressure of the cinches, she shook herself like a dog and snorted gratefully. Presently she was cropping at bunch grass in great content, as beautiful a creature as one would find in many and many a day of hard hunting.

Mr. Yeager hobbled up to the mare and laid his hand on her shoulder that shone like metal in the morning light.

"Ah," said he, "she's a beauty, though! She's a beauty, ain't she, Tommy?"

"She is," said Tommy.

"You paid a pretty good price for her eh?" said the old man.

"Well," murmured Grant, "a good deal more than you're asking for the saddle to put on her."

"Is *that* so? Well, sir, she's a fine mare and a comfort to a man that knows hossflesh—but she ain't the hoss that can wear my saddle!"

13

Grant stared incredulously at the other. Then he flashed an angry glance at Tommy.

"Have you brought me up here to make a fool of me and the mare?" he asked.

"I told you what would happen," said Tommy calmly. "I didn't invite you to try to get the saddle."

"In a word," said Grant, "you only pretend that you want to sell the saddle, but as a matter of fact you would never part with it!"

Mr. Yeager smiled upon the other without irritation. "Young man," said he to Grant, "I used to ask three thousand dollars for this here same saddle—and a hoss that suited me to put the saddle on. In them days a lot of men used to come along and try for the saddle. There was plenty that raked up three thousand out of the cattle or gold or lumber or a lucky night at cards. And a lot of 'em had good hosses, too!

"There was Ches Langer that went clean all the way to Kentucky and blowed in twenty-five hundred dollars on a pretty slick piece of hossflesh. That was nine years ago, when prices in hossflesh wasn't what they are now. Ches came back here with a jim-dandy—a regular flash of a hoss, that was.

You was only a kid, then, but I guess that you remember, Tommy!''

"I tell a man I do!"

"The ends of that hoss was better than any picture that you ever seen, stranger. He had shoulders and neck and head on him that couldn't be better. But in the middle he looked sort of soft. *Too* much like a picture. So I says to Ches: 'Ride that hoss to Peter Lang's house and back by tomorrow this time.' That was about eighty miles—and eighty miles of hard going. However, that was the sort of work that a man could expect out of the sort of a hoss that would be fit to wear this saddle.

"Ches, he made a face, but he pulled out on the trail without sayin' nothing. He rode all the way to Lang's and half an hour before time was up the next day, he come back. He had made the trip in only fifteen hours, and then he stopped off near my place and rubbed his hoss down and give it a feed and tried to coax it into good condition. But nothin' would do, and when he rode that hoss up to me, the critter was all ganted up. It didn't have no belly at all.

"And I says to Ches: 'I don't want a hoss that's fine for Kentucky; I want a hoss that's fine for mountain work!'

"Ches didn't answer me back none. He just went off grievin'. And so it goes. I've dropped the price to twenty-five hundred and then two thousand; then fifteen hundred and finally a thousand, so's to let in more hosses. But still I don't seem to see no real hossflesh in these here days. The old breeds, they've died out, I guess!''

"What's wrong with the mare?" asked Harry Grant, scowling, as he lighted one of his black cigars.

"She's a good mare—a pretty thing—fast and pretty slick all over. But she ain't up to carryin' weight."

"How do you know that?"

"By the cut of her, I know it. Ain't it true?"

Mr. Grant was sullenly silent.

"Besides," said Yeager gently, "she ain't just right in one of the forelegs. She'll let you down in front, one of these days, won't she?"

Mr. Grant showed that after all he was not really a bad loser by breaking into a cordial laughter and clapping his hands together. "You people," he declared, "can read the mind of a horse. I admit that you're right, Yeager. The mare has that one flaw. As for the weight carrying, I don't know. But I suppose that you know horseflesh better than I know it—or guess it! But where will you ever find a horse that will satisfy you?"

"I've seen it, once!" said the old man. "When I was a kid, a mighty little kid, me and my pa were out riding and we seen a bay mustang stallion come flarin' over a hill. He seen us and come up standin', with his mane shakin' up and his eyes ragin' at us, like he despised us a lot more than he feared us.

"Well, he stood there a minute, lookin' more like a thing out of heaven than a thing raised on grass and meanness. Then he shot back over the hill, and we never seen him no more. When he was gone we didn't speak to each other for a time, and then my dad says to me: 'Willy, men is ornery, good-for-nothin' critters, ain't they?'

"And I said that they was. The very next week, dad started workin' on this saddle. When he died he left me his plans and his drawin', and I kept on at it. But though we never talked about it, we had the same idea. It was the glimpse of that stallion and the picture of him that made us keep workin' at the leather carvin'.

"Well, sir, that was a famous hoss. Red Lightnin' they called him. And when I see a hoss that ain't so good as him but that even reminds me of him, then I'll cut down my price another notch to see my saddle on that hoss's back!"

Mr. Grant listened with much respect. But he understood now the meaning of Porter's Hagan. And he looked narrowly at Tommy, who said:

"I've brought up a hoss for you to look at, Will Yeager."

"And how much money?" asked Will incredulously.

"A thousand dollars."

"In promises?"

"In cash!"

"Dog-gone me, Tommy, have you started to be a workin' man?" He peered at the youngster and then added gloomily: "Nope, you'll never be that. It ain't in you, son! It ain't in you!"

He added sharply: "Lemme see the hoss that is to take this here saddle away from me!"

"You have to give up the saddle *some* day!" suggested the boy mildly.

"Don't I know that?" snapped the old man. "Don't I know that? But lemme see your hoss! Where is it? That nag yonder?"

For answer, Tommy whistled high and sharp, and suddenly from the trees flashed the form of Porter's Hagan, swerving down the slope. Some distant sound or sight checked it in mid-career. It halted on stiffly planted legs. The long mane tumbled over Hagan's ears, and the tail flirted across the satin body of the horse like a play of fire across polished steel.

"Ah!" murmured old Will Yeager. He turned his back and laid his hand on the shoulder of Tommy and leaned there with his eyes closed, breathing hard. "Ah, there he is again!"

"It's no ghost," said Tommy. "A black horse this time, Will Yeager."

"Leave him be! Leave him be a minute, and then I'll look him over. But if they's a flaw in him, out he goes and the saddle stays with me!"

So, presently, Tommy sat cross-legged on a stone directly in front of the stallion and looked into his eye and saw there the cold glimmerings of danger when the old man touched Hagan. But when the danger signal flew, a single word repressed it, and once more Hagan stood like a lamb and, with his ears flickering back and forth, endured that examination.

The black cigar of Mr. Grant was consumed to the butt; another was lighted and slowly smoked away before the examination was finished. He saw the stallion walk and trot and gallop, before Will was satisfied. At length, the old man turned to Tommy Mayo and said:

"Tommy, you ain't got no business to have a hoss like that."

"Why not, Will?"

"Because it'll carry you into a lot of trouble!"

"I'll take the trouble. Do I get the saddle?"

"Aye, son, you get the saddle!"

In a trice, it was swung upon the back of Hagan, and the stallion stood before them, transformed.

"And the bridle?" asked Tommy, as he counted a thousand dollars into the hand of the old man.

"The bridle, too? Aye, he needs that, also!"

It was a solid mass of silver, so it seemed. It gleamed like strips of ice upon the head and against the black hide of the horse, and under the chin there was a faint sound of bells, so delicate that it was no louder than the voice of insects which men hear when the wind dies.

Tommy sprang into the saddle. "Will," said he, "will you wish me luck?"

"I'll wish it to you," said Will, "but that black hoss never carried a man to good luck before and I doubt that he'll start new habits now! So long, Tommy. So long, stranger. Tommy, how many gents are gunna try to rip your throat open for the sake of that bit of leather that you're ridin' on!"

So Tommy swept away at the side of Grant.

"But is your horse so fast, after all?" asked Grant suddenly, thinking of the advantage his lighter weight gave to him. "Do you think that you could run away from me?"

"Try me!" Tommy grinned. "Down the hollow and up the farther side."

"You may beat me to the hollow," said Grant shrewdly, "but I'll be at the top of the next rise before you!"

"Will you bet on that?"

"As much as you please."

"I have only two hundred and fifty dollars," said Tommy with another grin.

"That's enough. We're off!"

The head of the stallion was turned, and so was his body,

when Mr. Grant seized upon this favorable opportunity to start. He flung the little mare like an arrow down the slope. The gale which her gallop raised was roaring in the ears of Harry Grant, as he whirled to the bottom of the slope. Still the black stallion had not overtaken them. And now before them there was nothing but the slope where his lighter weight would tell mightily in his behalf.

Up the slope he went, now, the mare working with all her heart, her ears flattened and her body, from the tip of her nose to the tip of her tail, making a straight line. With the sway of his body and the blows of his whip, jockeying her with all of a very great skill, Mr. Grant drew from Dolly the last atom of her speed.

Halfway to the top, she wavered a little to the side. And past her rushed Hagan with great, careless bounds; past her, and up the slope, with Tommy turned in the saddle and smiling back!

14

It might be said truthfully that Mr. Grant was not a man of foolish pride. But on this occasion he knew that he had a great pull in the weights, a start that left his enemy standing still, the advantage of a very light saddle whose short stirrups enabled him to throw his weight forward and swing rhythmically with the mare in her stride. In addition, he had the consciousness that Dolly, tough and true as she was in a distance run, was preeminently qualified to shine as a sprinter—and the course of this run was short!

In spite of all of these advantageous truths, here was the black horse running as carelessly as a colt taking the morning air, yet sweeping past the mare with a huge twenty-five-foot stride that made her seem like a pounding pony in comparison. It stung Mr. Grant, for, if he were nothing else, he was at least a horseman, and he knew horseflesh! He knew, first of all, that Dolly was as neat a trick as he had ever sat astride of. And here she was, turned into a ridiculous imitation of a real horse, by comparison.

The black was so far ahead at the top of the hill that Tommy had drawn him back to what was little more than a hand gallop; even so—such was the tremendous stretch and swing of the stallion—Dolly had all she could do to keep beside him. She had never run more smoothly, never run truer or fleeter. But when Grant turned his eye upon the stallion he saw that glorious animal sweeping along and flicking the earth with the tips of his hoofs, so to speak—an effortless, quite amazing gallop!

To his great chagrin, Mr. Grant was forced to call for mercy, and Tommy brought the stallion to a trot, an easy, gliding trot. Hagan's supple fetlock joints dipped almost to the earth, and Tommy seemed to be sitting in a boat. Dolly, by dint of maintaining a steady gallop, kept at the side of the black beauty.

"Well," said Grant at last, "you have the horse, it seems."

"I never doubted that," said Tommy. "And I have two hundred and fifty extra, at that!"

Mr. Grant scowled. He could not help it; not that he was a poor loser, but it still seemed absurd that any horse could have accepted such a handicap and given the mare such a ludicrous beating. However, he paid over the lost bet.

"Do you see that white rock on the top of the hill, yonder?" said young Tommy as he tucked the money into his pocket.

"I see it."

"I'll give you and the mare a hundred yards and then beat you to that rock."

"For the fun of it?"

"For five hundred dollars, Mr. Grant."

"The devil you will! I'll never bet agin' that black scoundrel again. There is too much sense in his hoofs! Tell me, Tommy, how that old man has been able to keep such a saddle as that without having it stolen?"

"It's been stolen six times, at least," said Tommy. "Six times, and still it has come back to Will Yeager each time."

"He's been able to trail the thieves each time?"

"He doesn't need to. That saddle is known in every town near this place—a hundred miles or more from it. And when the saddle is seen, people start asking questions. They know what Will's idea of a horse is."

"Will they ask the same questions of you?"

"They'll see Hagan, and that ought to be enough."

"Where now?" asked Grant.

"We're on the trail of that rifle and those revolvers that I told you of."

"Far away?"

"Five miles more."

"And after that?"

"Then we follow your trail as far as you please and where you please, until you have nothing more to teach me."

"Have I much, then?" asked Grant, still sulky.

"You have enough. For instance—why doesn't a gun show on you?"

"Because sometimes I meet a fool who thinks that I *haven't* a gun merely because I don't show one. And at the worst, when I meet a real gunfighter, he will make his draw a split part of a second slower because he is pretty sure that I can't get the guns out of my clothes as fast as he can get them out of his holsters."

"But can you?" asked Tommy.

"Fast enough, I think. A holster may be a shade quicker, but guns from beneath the armpits are more surprising. And surprise is half of a fight, I suppose!"

Tommy nodded.

"You agree?" asked Grant.

"I agree with anything you say," said Tommy. "You're the teacher!"

Mr. Grant looked almost sadly upon his youthful companion. "How many lives will you take when you learn how to handle a gun a little better than you handle it now?"

"If I learn to use the tricks you know, Mr. Grant," said he, "I hope that I'll get such a reputation that I won't have to spill five drops in five years."

"You'll make them drop with your name alone?" Harry Grant grinned.

"That can be done," said this assured youth. "Here's a bad bit of going. Don't follow me unless you want to!"

As he said this, young Tommy turned from their course and led through a screen of shrubbery to the edge of a valley whose sloping wall was pitching down at a sharp angle toward the bottom of the ravine. A stream, yellow with mud or white with froth, rushed down the center of the hollow. A narrow bridge staggered across the stream, and on the farther side, near the bridge, was a little house not much more pretentious than the one in which the leather carver had been living.

"Do you mean," said Grant, "that you really intend to ride down that cliff?"

"I mean that."

"You are a dead man, then," said Grant.

"I have money in my pocket that will say I intend to live."

Grant smiled without mirth. "If you win, I'll be out some more money," said he. "If you lose, I have only to go down and pick your pocket in order to get everything that you own. So why should I make the bet?"

Tommy shot a single glance at his new friend, and that single glance traveled a long distance toward the hidden soul of Mr. Grant.

However, he did not pause to argue, but he sent the black stallion forward to the edge of the cliff. Indeed, it was hardly less than a sheer precipice. The black horse paused with a snort, and dropping his head sharply, he sniffed in the air as though the wind that crossed the valley were telling him of the danger that lived in that descent.

In the interval Mr. Grant asked gently: "How do you get fine guns from a shack like this in the midst of the wilderness, Tommy?"

"There's a fellow down there who is a gunsmith," said Tommy. "Cringle is his name. He's got a way of working on a gun until it has such a good balance that it can talk for itself. It hops out into your hand—Conrad Black carried a Cringle gun. This one!"

He drew a revolver and showed it. "There's nothing in the world like a set of guns that he has down there in his house. I suppose that the rifle is a new thing in its own line. You can handle it like a revolver, almost, it has such balance! And the revolvers are feathers—that's all. Besides, they're touched up with a little gold. So that two hundred and fifty for the set of three isn't so high."

"No," said the other. "I can see why it isn't so high. But why haven't others come along to buy the guns?"

"Those that have enough coin haven't enough skill in shooting."

"The devil! Is there a catch in the sale of these guns as there was in the sale of the horse?"

"Just that. There's a couple of catches. Old Cringle has a three-wire fence out there behind his house and the wires are stretched loose all the time. Well, if you have the two hundred and fifty dollars in the first place, in the second place you have to step out behind the house, take one of the revolvers and chop off the three wires at thirty yards in three seconds. Which isn't so easy, because after you've cut the first strand of wire in two, you have to blaze away at two remaining wires which are bobbing up and down a bit."

"Right!" said Grant. "But I think that it might be done."

"You could do it. And maybe I can do it. There are a good many others who might cut the wires by luck or just by skill. But there's another thing that keeps them back."

"Well?"

"That's the Cringle boys. The pair of them have been working all of their lives to get two hundred and fifty, and steady hands to cut those wires. Because the both of them want those guns. But when they have the money, they can't shoot straight, and when they're in trim for shooting, they haven't the cash. They've spent about five years, now, doing not much but trying to get those guns and keep off the rest of the world from their father's house. You can lay to it that one of 'em is somewhere around watching the road."

"So that's why you want to cut down the wall of the valley, like this!"

"I hate trouble!" admitted Tommy blandly—and then he winked most expressively at Harry Grant.

"But the other one may be waiting for you in the house, Tommy!"

"A fellow has to take a few chances, you know!"

With that, he dipped Hagan over the edge of the bluff, and the next moment there was a rattling of gravel, a thin-blowing cloud of dust with the glistening form of the stallion flashing through. Then yonder galloped Hagan over the floor of the valley. And down the valley wall there was still a trickle of stones which had been loosened when the great horse slid down.

Mr. Grant had not time to relax after this feat which he had witnessed, for now he saw the black horse driven at full speed straight toward the bank of the creek—as though Tommy, having escaped destruction riding down the perilous cliff, now courted it in the waters of the stream.

15

The teeth of Mr. Grant met through the cigar which, as usual, was in his mouth. His eyes bulged. The tobacco smoke rolled up into them and stung them sharply. But Harry Grant paid no attention to that. He saw the stallion raised into the air. He saw the edge of the bank, from which he sprang, crumble away and a huge bite of loosened earth and rock drop into the bed of the foaming creek.

But there was Hagan, hanging between earth and heaven with the sun glorious upon him. And there was the rider poised in the saddle like a bird upon the wing, and now they rushed down. They struck. For an instant he saw the big horse waver—so narrow was the chance—but then, recovering himself, he scrambled out onto the level beyond.

Mr. Grant wiped the perspiration from his brow as he watched the youth dismount and then enter into the shack.

It was more than a shack, now. It was like an ogre's den, and Harry Grant was fairly well assured that remarkable as he had found Tommy hitherto, that youth was apt to fail to return from the house of Mr. Cringle.

In the meantime, peace had been restored in the valley, and the fish hawk, which had been disturbed by the wild passage of Hagan across the valley, now dropped again out of the pale heart of the sky and steered up and down the course of the stream on magic wings.

Peace was restored, and the heart of Grant grew more quiet, as he could hear again the faintly stirring voices which lived in the wind. Grasshopper, frog, fly, bee, and distant bird, all had parts in that chorus.

Old women and young poets are pleased by that music of nature, but Mr. Grant was not pleased by it. It made him look sharply over either shoulder as though the still voices out of the air were telling him that danger approached stealthily, constantly behind him. He listened and believed. Then he said to himself:

"If a bullet went through my head, now, the second that the echoes were dead, all these whispers in the air would continue again. Harry Grant would be lying here dead, and what man or woman in the world would care whether or not I lived or died?"

So brooded Mr. Grant as he sat his horse near the edge of the cliff and fiddled uneasily at the bridle reins. And how long, how long he had fought them off! Surely there must be times when they despaired of any eventual success against him—all his enemies! Now he was buckling to his side an ally stronger than steel—if the young fool did not get his head shot off before he had a real chance to prove himself useful again!

Out of the heart of the valley, like a hollow voice calling from a deep well, the sounds of three shots rose to the attentive ear of Mr. Grant.

What had happened? Were the wires clipped? Those three shots were as evenly spaced as the ticking of a clock. Certainly Tommy had used his three seconds to the full! Mr. Grant raised his field glasses and drilled them upon the house just in time to see a hasty rider plunge from the trees on the near side of the little bridge and gallop his horse across it.

It seemed to Grant that, even from that distance, he could see the bridge reel and stagger under the weight of the big man and his big mount. Here was one of the Cringle sons, rushing home to learn the result of the last test on the wires of the father.

The result?

The door of the shack was cast open. Out stepped Tommy with a rifle under his arm. He swung into the saddle on the stallion. The white head of an old man glistened in the sunshine close to the door of the house. But here was the rescuer wheeling around the corner of the house. What would happen?

Mr. Grant saw the flash of young Cringle's revolver. It was like a tiny spark of light, such as glints at a distance, from a single wet leaf when the morning sun strikes against the forest. Then the form of Tommy and Hagan darted in between.

What happened, Harry Grant could not tell, but he knew that there was no glimmer of a weapon in the hands of Tommy. It seemed that, as he passed the big youth on the big horse, Tommy must have struck the stranger with his naked fist and struck him with a terrible force, to be sure. The latter threw his arms wide, dropped his gun, and toppled slowly out of the saddle into the arms of his father, while his horse leaped wildly from beneath him in pursuit of Hagan.

As well pursue the gleam of the marsh light! Yonder was Hagan at the bridge. There he was lost in the forest. There he reappeared halfway up the slope. Suddenly he had started forth at the side of Grant once more, so that it seemed the veriest dream that the black stallion could have been in the heart of the valley only the instant before. Only the heavy breathing of the black horse told such a tale.

The only comment of Grant—for he did not wish to turn the head of this youth by expressing surprise at every action— was to stretch out his arm and ask for a glimpse of the rifle. But Tommy shook his head.

"I know what it means," said he. "After you handled it, you'd begin to want it. And after you began to want it, you'd never be able to get it all out of your head. It would keep stuck in there like a burr. You would wake up in the middle of the night and think of that gun. And the revolvers the same way. It is a good deal better for you to keep away from them—and keep off the back of Hagan. But Hagan will take care of himself; the guns can't do that!''

Mr. Grant, saying nothing, thought the more. They looked quietly at one another, until Tommy yawned and glanced away. When they started on, however, the choice of the road was left to Grant, and he took the way at a round pace. They passed rapidly out of the highlands and with the approach of evening they were in the foothills and heading steadily east.

It was not yet dusk. The sun was down; the west was brilliant, and the lights of a little crossroads village before them were just beginning to twinkle feebly. Broad day was still upon the higher mountains; twilight was in the valleys. And through this light which showed one everything except the smallest features, Grant watched a horseman swing at an easy gallop past them heading west.

After the man had passed, Grant recognized that slanting seat and something haphazard in the whole bearing of the stranger. He said hurriedly to Tommy:

''Ride on. Go straight for the town and amuse yourself. I'll come in after you in a little while.''

Tommy, with a nod, loosened the rein, and Hagan was off like a bolt—instantly out of sight over the edge of the hill. Grant turned and pushed straight back down the trail at a sweeping pace. No doubt Dolly could not match gaits with Hagan, but at least she was able to walk in on any other horse that Grant had ever seen on the range.

The present one was no exception. He gained hand over hand and presently he saw the outline of the rider blurred in the night before him—still riding aslant in the unforgettable manner, careless, at peace with the world.

The rein of Dolly was loosened for the closing burst, and she cut away the last bit of distance with a sprint. It brought a volley of hoofbeats in the ear of the stranger, making him shorten rein and glance hastily over his shoulder. It was much too late, by that time, for the gun was in the hand of Harry Grant.

One glimpse of him was enough for the other. He passed his right hand to the butt of his revolver—but when he had measured the distance between him and the rushing form of Grant, he seemed to realize that, at such a distance, the latter could not miss. The man's hand came away again, and he sat the saddle with his left hand holding the reins and the right resting on the pommel.

Mr. Grant reined in Dolly with a savage suddenness. He was so close that his revolver was perilously close to the ribs of the other.

"Well met again, Barney!" said he.

Barney said nothing at all. He merely poked at his hat with a forefinger and so pushed the sombrero farther back on his head.

"At least," said Grant tauntingly, "I thought that there would be more fight in Barney."

"Give me thirty yards and an even break for my gun—and I'll take my chance," said the other.

"Is it a good chance?" Grant sneered.

"A cursed poor chance, of course," said Barney. "Nobody has a good chance against you, I suppose. Unless there's a new man in the mountains."

"There's a new man," admitted Grant, "but he's on my side. And that's why I rode after you this evening, Barney, instead of simply dropping you out of the saddle at the first sight."

"Well," said Barney, "I wondered what was in your head. Except that if you got rid of me, there would be a hundred more ready to take my place."

"Do you think so? But you're wrong! The boys are getting sick of it. They've been after me for a long time and they've had poor luck. Oh, mighty poor luck! They're beginning to grow tired of the work. Admit it, Barney!"

Barney shook his head. "I've kept on your trail for five

years, off and on. And I'm merely getting warmed up to the work.''

"Why do you dare to tell me that?" snarled Grant.

"Because you've had your killing for one day. O'Neil is one dead man for you! You'll want no more for a while!

So the news had spread so fast! It was already far down here among the hill villages.

"Ah," said Mr. Grant, "these aren't the good old days! A man could depend on a bit of time and a good many miles in the old days. But the telephone does the trick now. The wires are tangled all through the mountains. I wish they were in Hades—who strung them!"

"Does it make your knees sag a little?"

"No!"

"You're not so cool as you used to be," said Barney. "Not quite so cold-blooded. I suppose that even Grant is weakening, eh?"

"Barney, why don't I finish you because of your cursed impudence? Shall I let you live to try to shoot me in the back some other day?"

"Do as you please," said Barney. "It's a small thing to me! And there are others in the crowd who feel like me. Finish me while you have the chance. But I swear to you, Grant, that if one of us ever gets you with your back to the wall, there'll be no foolish mercy for you."

"I know that," said the other slowly. "Oh, I know all of that. You'd cut my throat with a smile."

"As you cut O'Neil's today."

"What made you think that it was I?"

"Who else would it be?"

"Suppose that I tell you that you're wrong?"

"Say what you please. Only tell me this, Grant: Is it true that you've found another man to trust you—*you*?"

He spoke it with such an accent of horror that Grant twisted in the saddle and gasped: "Am I a snake?"

"Never mind," said Barney. "But only tell me if it's true?"

"The next time that you or some of the rest try for me, you'll find out for yourself! So long, Barney. If I stay here talking to you much longer, I'll put a slug into you. Ride along!"

Barney, without a word of answer, turned the head of his horse and cantered obediently down the road. It was thick of the dusk, now, but through the dull light the gunman could see the tilt of Barney's body in the saddle. And he remembered other days, when Barney and he had ridden side by side on wild errands, each with a perfect trust in the other, each with the confidence that a veritable army of faithful strength was cantering at his side.

So Grant turned back down the road where the village lights twinkled faint and far in the hollow, and the thoughts of the dead days went like ghosts beside him.

16

He found a crowd of people in front of the hotel. There were half a dozen lanterns, and they cast a very bright light upon the central figure around which the circle was thronging. That figure was Hagan, and upon the back of Hagan was the empty saddle which had come from the hands of Will Yeager on that day.

There were boys and there were women in the crowd, and their numbers were constantly increasing. As the rumor went up or down the street, new recruits hurried out of houses, away from half-finished suppers and came running to see the new wonder. But the women and the children made no sound. They merely huddled and swayed with the rest of the crowd, pressing strongly and silently in, to gain better posts of vantage so that they might pore upon the new attraction.

It was the men who did the speaking. What they spoke of was the saddle first—the horse afterward.

Everyone in the town seemed to know all about that saddle. Now and then some one of the men made an attempt to get closer to the stallion to take the saddle from its back. All such efforts were useless. Hagan, with flattened ears and head pointing straight ahead, kept shifting his hind quarters just enough from side to side to enable him to keep a complete view of the circle of watchers. The instant that the least movement was made toward him, he lashed out with a deadly pair of heels.

Hagan had already got in his first stroke of mischief. Yonder on the veranda of the hotel there was one poor fellow groaning. For many a minute he had not spoken at all after the blow had fallen, for he had been the first to approach the black horse, and his fate had warned the rest of what might happen. The darting heels of Hagan had grazed his head and put him flat on his back with the crimson streaming down his face.

That was not the only sound from the veranda of the hotel. Another man, entirely heedless of the groans of his neighbor and of all the disturbance which was pooled around the horse, was blowing a gay, light air upon his flute. Mr. Grant smiled when he heard the music!

"What's wrong?" he asked the nearest man who was edging in on the border of the crowd.

"Someone has stolen Yeager's saddle, again. And the fool brought it right into town and left it on his horse!"

"Did he?" asked Grant. "But what if he really owns the saddle?"

"Is that hoss worth bein' under such a saddle? Didn't I see the bay hoss that Gregory tried and that old man Yeager turned down? That was a *hoss*! Why, this black hoss, here, ain't no more than a cheapskate alongside of it."

It was plain that the saddle had become a superstition in the mountains; people would continue to ask many questions whenever they saw horse and saddle together. Here were women holding up their children and trying to point out the wonderful designs which were carved in the leather.

"Because most like you ain't never gunna have a chance to see that saddle or anything like it in the rest of your life!"

Mr. Grant, listening, was inclined to agree with them.

"Where's the man who rode the hoss into town?" he asked.

"He came in sometime this evening."

"Nobody saw him?"

"Only two or three. Most folks were at table having their supper."

"If he stole the saddle, would he dare to bring it into the town?"

"Not knowing that everybody knew it, stranger. Besides, this gent may of took it for granted that nobody would pay any attention in the dark. It was the storekeeper that happened to put his eye on it. He's so used to seeing cheats that he don't miss nothing even at midnight!"

He laughed heartily at this feeble joke.

"Will the saddle be taken off the horse?" asked Grant, a little amused and a little alarmed, also.

"It sure will!"

The alarm of Grant increased. For he had an idea that before the saddle was taken off, a man-sized hurricane would descend upon that crowd.

"How will they find out if the saddle is truly owned by the stranger?" he asked again.

"They're trying to get in touch with Yeager. They've phoned up to a house nigh onto his, and the word will be carried across to him, I guess. We'll know pretty soon and—hey, here comes the news now!"

"Well," a voice from the hotel veranda was shouting, "well, we've got word through from Yeager!"

"Did he sell the saddle?" came the shout.

"He sold the saddle!"

There was a groan of interest.

"To whom?"

"A bird named Tommy Mayo."

"Where is he?"

"Look around! Where's the fellow who rode in on this black colt? It's a black hoss, all right, that this Tommy Mayo rode. Who's Tommy Mayo?"

"I never heard of him."

Then a loud voice came from the veranda of the hotel:
"Hello, kid! Ain't you the one that rode the hoss and the
saddle into town?"

The music of the flute had ceased. Mr. Grant listened with
great interest to the voice that replied—the drawling, lazy
voice of Tommy.

"I'm the one that brought the hoss in. Yes!"

"Then why didn't you speak up?"

The lanterns were being hurried in the direction of the
speakers and Mr. Grant saw the first sketchy outlines of
Tommy's figure.

"Speak up when?"

"When you heard them asking for Tommy Mayo!"

"D'you think that *I'm* Tommy Mayo?"

"Why not?"

"Old-timer," said Tommy, "maybe you dunno what sort
of a gent Tommy Mayo is?"

The lanterns were gathered close, now, and Tommy was
revealed brightly to all the crowd of townsmen. He stood at
ease in all that glare and listened to the general exclamation:

"Tell us about this Tommy Mayo."

"I'll tell you," said Tommy. "When *he* comes to town
you'll know about it. Tommy Mayo? Why, friends, d'you
think that he'd come to you dressed up in old togs like these
ones?"

He laughed heartily at that absurd notion. "He'd come
looking like a gold mine," said Tommy. "That's how he'd
come!"

"Where did you get that horse, then, if you're not young
Mayo?"

"He told me to take the horse into town, here. He had
something else to do. Besides, he wants me to give a warning
to some of the folks in the town, here. He wants to warn Sid
Channing and Lew Morrissey. He wants me to tell them that
he's coming and that he's after their scalps. Y'understand?
He says that when he *does* come into town, he's going to get
after them both and get after them quick. So if any of you are

friendly to them two, I guess that you'd better tell them to oil up their guns."

"Hello, Morrissey! He's talking about you. Step up and listen to him."

A tall, slender man with long, blond mustaches strode onto the veranda and stood loftily above young Tommy.

"What might your name be, kid?" he asked.

"Jones," replied Tommy.

"This Tommy Mayo—that I never heard tell of before— you say that he's on my trail?"

"So he says."

"For what, will you tell me that?"

"If you want to crawl out of the fight," said Tommy, "I guess that he won't hound you none."

There was a gasp from the crowd at such a speech. Apparently Morrissey was a known man.

"I'll crawl out of no fight," said Mr. Morrissey. "If this Tommy Mayo remembers me better than I remember him, I'll be right here ready and waiting for him! Tommy Mayo— cursed if I ever heard of the name before!"

He retreated, with a very thoughtful face, and in the general murmur which followed—a low-pitched stir of earnest voices in which there was only the double challenge as a theme—Mr. Grant found a chance to draw Tommy to one side.

"What in the name of heaven are you doing, Tommy?" he asked.

"Making a name for myself."

"Or digging a grave, maybe."

"Maybe that."

"What do you mean by introducing yourself with yourself? They'll laugh you out of the town when you show your face again!"

"They have a flash of me by lantern light—in these dirty old togs. But when they see me again, I'll be a flash. That two fifty that I got from you has to be sunk in clothes, in the meantime. When do we leave town?''

''Now, if you wish to.''

''The sooner the better.''

In ten minutes they were beyond the village. And in ten minutes more, they were lying in their blanket rolls with the trees above them and the scent of the pines drenching the air until their throats tingled at every inhalation.

''Tommy,'' said the other, ''is this the way you're to work with me? Getting yourself salted away with lead? And—what the devil have Morrissey and Sid Channing ever done to you?''

''Nothing.''

''What!''

''Not a thing.''

''Are you mad?''

''Morrissey,'' said Tommy, ''is the worst crook that ever put a leg over a saddle—unless Channing is as bad. I don't know. The pair of them work together, and they're a rosy set, I'll tell a man!''

''And you've ridden into this town to insult a pair of men who are dangerous, but who were never dangerous to you.''

''I have to have a reputation,'' said Tommy. ''Otherwise I'll be of no use to you. If they kill me—that's the end of me and my story. If I have to stand up and kill them, there'll be no loss to the world. But what I'm gambling on is that the pair of them will be worried to death when they hear that I'm coming back, and they'll sneak out of town beforehand. If they do, that will be a feather in my cap.''

''What makes you think that they'll run from you?''

''*Because* they've never heard of me. That's the reason. They're crooks—black crooks. And that's why they'll back down, I think. If they knew something about me, it would be different.''

''So you gamble on that?''

''I do!''

''What are you going to do now?''

"Go to the next town, rig myself up in fine togs, and get ready for a flashy entrance into the town again. And I'll send the word before me that Tommy Mayo is coming. Reputation, Mr. Grant! That's what I've got to make and then capitalize!"

Mr. Grant did not attempt further argument. He merely curled himself up in his blankets and watched the wavering blackness of the trees above him, with a star pricking through the shadows, here and there. At last, sleep began to creep over him—not the vague, nervous, restless fear of oblivion which had been with him for so many months, but a perfect trust that the man at his side was a watchman who would keep his life safe!

He slept—without dreams, heavily, like a child. When he wakened, it was the prying hand of the morning light against his eyelids that disturbed him, and no sound. Fifty yards away, through a gap among the trees, he saw a thin blue column of smoke rising. There was Tommy preparing breakfast adroitly. The two horses grazed side by side in the little clearing beyond. The sun showered down upon them. A busy jay was speaking out of the bright distance of the morning, and Mr. Grant felt that he had entered upon a life of secure peace at last!

17

Busy days for both of them followed. Mr. Harry Grant was willing enough to interrupt his plans and his journeys in order to make up lost time in sleep and lazy hours of rest during the day. But he was not allowed this luxury, for during the day Tommy Mayo demanded attention.

The languor seemed to fall like a cloak from Tommy. From dawn to dark he was busily at work, and the secret which was being mastered under the tuition of Harry Grant was none other than the complicated matter of drawing a gun from one's clothes with as much speed as a weapon can be snatched from a holster by the most expert hand. So, with gun slings arranged under his armpits and inside the belt of his trousers, Tommy labored steadily.

There was much to be taught to him, and he listened and absorbed the instruction of Mr. Grant with a hungry ear. Five minutes of demonstration—and then Tommy would retire to the shadows of the woods to practice patiently what he had learned. After that, he would return, just as Grant was sinking into a profound sleep, for a new demonstration from the master.

"And when I have taught you everything," said Grant at

last, "how do I know that you won't use all my knowledge against me, someday?"

"Because," said Tommy, "you and I will realize that we'll make only very bitter pills for one another to swallow! I think we'll keep clear of poison when we know it!"

With this, Harry Grant could not but agree. For five days the teaching continued. On the afternoon of the fifth day, Tommy disappeared and did not appear again on his black horse until the next morning. Harry Grant, gloomily bending over the breakfast fire, half convinced that his youthful protégé had deserted him forever, felt a shadow trail swiftly across the farthest corner of his field of vision. He looked up in haste to see a flashing picture of cowboy brilliancy galloping toward him.

The two hundred and fifty dollars, it seemed, had been invested totally in this costume. There was enough flash of sheer gold alone to suggest an even greater sum—from the metal work that surrounded the sombrero to the arched flash of the spurs. The sheen of a blue jay's feathers was matched in the brilliant silk which Tommy wore, and nothing but the rich, red orange of dying coals could match the flaming silken scarf which was knotted around his throat.

Under his right knee there was the long holster which contained the rifle of old Cringle. But the two Cringle revolvers were nowhere in sight. They were sheathed out of view in the clothes of Tommy, and in spite of their bulk, not a hint of a lump appeared. The flute was at the lips of this cavalier, but blown so softly that the stir of the wind through the trees had been enough to drown the sound of it.

But now it came like a shrill whisper to the ears of Mr. Grant. It seemed to him, as he watched the rider pass like a rainbow flash through a spot of sun fallen through the lofty trees, that he was looking upon a transformation of human flesh.

It was not a person merely changed from the lazy lout of the Mayo farm. It was a man recreated. This odd thought lodged for an instant in the brain of Mr. Grant, but it never entirely left him thereafter.

When Tommy drew nearer he dismounted and walked like a strutting peacock around the fire.

"When the boys see those clothes, Tommy," said Grant, "you'll have a rough time of it."

"I'm advertising," declared Tommy. "And if I can't win, I must go down with a crash. But if I win at all, I must be known. They've got to talk about me, Mr. Grant. They've got to watch me closer than that squirrel is watching me from the branch of that pine tree, yonder."

He waved his hand as though to point, but the gesture brought into his finger tips, by magic, a heavy revolver brilliantly chased with gold. He fired. And the tiny body of the squirrel tumbled over and over through the air and landed upon the ground, a headless thing.

Mr. Grant glanced at the victim and then at the victor. The revolver had already disappeared.

"You've been practicing a good deal more than I thought, Tommy," said he. "That was a very smooth trick!"

"I've been practicing in my head," said Tommy. "It isn't the handwork only that counts, but the thinking about a thing, eh?"

"Explain."

"Why, if you make a draw once in five minutes and spend the time in between thinking about what you've done and how you made your mistakes, you'll improve a whole lot faster than if you just wear yourself out slinging a heavy gun around! So I've kept your gun plays in mind all the time. And now I almost have it, eh?"

"You almost have it," admitted Grant.

"But not quite," confessed Tommy. "Aye, that's the difference! Just a little off, still! But I can do it well enough to try my luck with the game. Eh?"

"What game?"

"I start for town today."

Mr. Grant shook his head, but he said nothing. After

breakfast he heard how Tommy had found the clothes that he wanted, and how he had dressed in them in the woods and how he had paraded himself down the morning road to the infinite amazement of a pair of cowpunchers in a nearby field. That tale was interrupted.

A beat of horse's hoofs on the road nearby roused Tommy. He was in the saddle in an instant and shot away on the black horse. Through a narrow rift in the trees, Mr. Grant peered after the other, and he saw Tommy start out onto the roadway and present himself suddenly before a horseman who was swinging away in a leisurely fashion, with the dust puffing up from the cantering hoofs of his mustang.

They were only an instant beside one another. Then Tommy was off through the trees again. The cowpuncher in the trail gazed after him for a moment; and then he began to ride again—but with a great difference. The prick of his spurs pitched the mustang straight up into the air with a squeal of pain and surprise, and then the little horse landed running and scooted out of view.

Tommy came laughing back to Harry Grant. He had given the stranger a message that he, Tommy Mayo, would that day appear in the town to find and punish the two ruffians, Morrissey and Channing. He would punish them, not only because they had ill used him, but because they had behind them the reputation of having ill used other men. The cowpuncher had listened to this message with a hungry interest and swore that he would deliver it word for word to both of the miscreants.

"And I wish you luck, kid!" he had said to Tommy. "They're an ornery pair!"

It was just after the hottest moment of the afternoon that Tommy decided to ride into the town because, as he explained to his companion, the nerves of the townsmen would have reached breaking point, by that time, and so, also, would the nerves of the two men whom he had challenged.

"When you get to lazying along through the hottest part of the day," said Tommy, "with something on your mind—why, that's the time that breaks your nerve! That's the time that starts all sorts of gents drinking when they're in a pinch! Maybe Morrissey and Channing have waited long enough to be sort of sick. I don't know!''

However eager Mr. Grant might be to see the fun, he did not care to ride into the town at the side of Tommy, for, as he explained to the latter, everytime he doubled back upon his trail he was apt to ride straight into the face of danger, since he could not tell how closely his enemies might be following him. What he proposed to do, therefore, was to approach the town across the hills, in a semicircle. Coming up behind the hotel building, he would gain some spot of vantage where he could see without being seen. And that was the plan which Grant executed. He shook hands with Tommy. ''I don't know whether or not I ought to wish you luck,'' said Grant. ''But I think that you'll have it!''

Then he sent Dolly scurrying away among the trees.

He came up, as he had expected, in the dead quiet of the day, between the hotel and the blacksmith shop, and leaving Dolly to graze on a patch of long bunch-grass, he advanced to a nest of old junk—wire, broken wheels of wagons and buggies—from which he could look up and down the street and there make sure that the stage was set for the appearance of the chief actor. But there could be no doubt at all that everything was well from the viewpoint of Tommy.

The town of Newbury was turned out en masse, and not only were the men banked solidly upon the hotel veranda, but the women were packed behind doors and windows of the houses on the opposite side of the street. The front of the blacksmith shop was flocked with spectators, also. For everyone seemed to take it for granted that the battle would take place in this central portion of the town.

On the whole, there was a heavy silence over Newbury. The very air was still, except that now and again the heat formed a current which was given the shape of a puff of wind that would suck up a drift of white dust, send it towering above the houses—and then, like a phantom, it jerked to pieces and disappeared before the eye.

Aside from those brief flurries, which raised a whispering sound, there was only the thin-edged buzzing of the flies, broken now and again by the booming flight of a bee or the savage whirring of a wasp. Far off, one of those jays, which are never absent when mischief is on foot, was talking in a harsh voice to a still more distant companion. But the people of Newbury waited with never a word. Harry Grant could stand it no longer.

"Are Morrissey and Channing sure to turn up for the fight?" he asked of the nearest among those in the blacksmith shop.

He spoke very gently, and yet the sound of his voice made all heads twitch around suddenly, and many eyes stared at him as though in scorn and anger.

"I dunno about Morrissey," said the nearest man, turning back to watch the street. "But there's Channing across the way, all ready and waiting!"

Mr. Grant looked in the designated direction. He saw a little man with hunched-up shoulders, sitting on a sadly shattered box, whittling calmly at a stick. It was Channing, no doubt. There was a significant open space around this man.

Yet the rapid movements of the knife in his slender fingers made Grant think of quite another man. Then the other looked up, and Harry Grant turned white.

18

It was not Channing. That was not the name which Grant knew for him. In the old days there had ridden at the side of Grant and the rest of his men a certain hard-fighting, straight, grim-hearted youth named Dick Ware. And this was Dick. There was in no place in the world another pair of bushy white eyebrows like Dick's. His face was as lean, as hollow-cheeked as ever; his eyes, when he looked up, were fully as active and as sure.

When he stared about him, almost the first thing that his glance fell upon was the form of Mr. Grant on the farther side of the street. Dick Ware started up. And the hand of Mr. Grant suddenly was pressed against his breast, where it clung in a sort of deprecatory gesture—like one who asks pardon!

From that position, his revolver was just exactly a tenth of a second from the exploding point. Perhaps Dick Ware realized this. Or perhaps something else went through his mind, for suddenly he took off his hat, waved it at Mr. Grant with a sardonic smile, and then sat down again.

It brought a volley of keen glances toward Grant. Public attention was so distasteful to him that he was on the verge of retreating when another attraction called all eyes in a new current down the street. A cowpuncher sang out, from the farther side of the hotel:

"Here he comes, ladies and gents. That's the one that called himself Tommy Mayo. I can tell him by his black hoss and his blue shirt. He looks like a circus, pretty near! That's the gent that talked to me this morning!"

There, sure enough, was the first gaudy flash of Mr. Tommy Mayo! He rode the black stallion and he rode him at a walk. Why? To be sure of his aim when the time for fighting came, one might have thought. Mr. Grant knew better. It was so that Hagan, fighting for his head, with his dancing and his prancing, could thoroughly show off the splendor of himself and of his master.

Now, as Tommy approached the center of the town, he dismounted and pronounced a word that transformed the stallion into a black statue. He advanced a little and took off his heavily loaded Mexican sombrero. The sun glittered on his well-slicked hair. He bowed to the crowd like an actor coming onto the stage.

The men were silent, still, but each man of Newbury shifted from foot to foot, and the result was a sound like a curious, hushed whisper. From across the street, also, there was another murmur, like a sigh. But it was not made by the mere rubbing of clothes against clothes. For yonder were the ladies of Newbury, old and young. And truly, Mr. Mayo made a gallant picture as he stood yonder in the sun!

He straightened again and replaced the hat—with a flash of its metal work—upon his head.

"I've come calling," said Tommy, "but I don't see the friends that were going to receive me here in Newbury. Will Morrissey and Channing step out and give me an eyeful of themselves?"

For the first time, one of the dangers to Tommy came into the mind of his waiting friend. For he recalled, now, that the face of Channing was quite unknown to young Mayo. It was a vast advantage from any point of view for Dick Ware—or whatever his true name might be!

Channing, alias Dick Ware, made no movement to step out and call attention to himself. The pressure of attention was beginning to fall upon him, however, and he must presently have met the challenge or have been shamed, when there was a sudden interruption which called all notice away from him.

Down the street a voice shouted, and Grant, glancing quickly in that direction, was aware of the tall form of Morrissey and the long glimmer of a rifle carried in his hands. A rifle for a street fight! There was something savage and unfair in this manner of warfare. However, there could be no rule against it. It afforded a sharp insight into the mind and the manners of Mr. Morrissey.

"Mayo!" cried Mr. Morrissey.

As he spoke, people dived from in front of him to get from the possible path of flying bullets. They had barely sufficient time. Half a dozen sprang to one side or another, and there was Mr. Morrissey revealed with his rifle at his shoulder and his forefinger curled upon the trigger. At the touch of his voice, as though operated by a spring, Tommy Mayo whirled, but who can turn his body in the time that it takes another to settle a rifle butt into the hollow of the shoulder?

Speed could never have saved Tommy, taken as he was from behind. But as he whirled he leaped sidewise, also. As the rifle spat, the bullet merely flicked through the shoulder of his coat. At the same instant, Tommy turned, and his revolver was in his hand. Even before most people had seen the flash of it they heard the report.

Then they saw Morrissey reel, fumble before him, and go down on one knee. There was still fighting spirit in the man, however. Perhaps he expected no mercy—or wanted none! There had been time for Tommy to follow his first shot with three more placed ones—but he stood with his revolver hanging at the length of his side, watching the other. And what he saw was Morrissey jerking the rifle to his shoulder once more, as he kneeled in the dust of the street!

The muzzle of the revolver jerked nervously up again—not so high as the level of the hip. It exploded in the hand of

Tommy, and Morrissey with a scream toppled onto the flat of his back. There he lay writhing and yelling.

The first bullet had merely sliced through the flesh of his leg, but the second shot had smashed the joint of his shoulder, making him a ruined man for life.

The street was in a commotion at once. It was not what had happened, for Newbury had seen many a shooting before this day. It was rather the manner of the happening that was of importance. Men in the midst of a gun fight do not ordinarily pause and wait for the other men, particularly when they have been assailed from behind.

Neither do they stand up straight and stiff like a duelist. But, throwing themselves in some position, which makes the smallest target, they pour forth shot on shot, as rapidly as their anxious fingers can work the gun, until one man or the other is silenced. Yet here was Tommy Mayo, who had held his fire with a wonderful deliberation while Morrissey, mad with venom, struggled to plant a return bullet in the body of the youth.

Here was Tommy, finally, who had saved himself in the nick of time with a second shot. And all so calmly and so surely done! What doubt is there in the mind of the eagle when, from his loftier stand in the air, he sees the fish hawk rising?

The street was now crowded with people swarming toward young Tommy Mayo. They wanted to shake his hand; they wanted to get close to him. They wanted to estimate all sorts of little things about him. Men wanted to guess at his weight and his age—and his honesty.

Channing, alias Dick Ware, was almost forgotten. The few glances which did travel in his direction did not find him. Dick had quietly disappeared in the first stir of the crowd—as though he had seen enough to convince him that Tommy Mayo was not a pleasant man for hand-to-hand conversation.

Mr. Harry Grant looked for Channing, also, and smiled broadly when he saw that the latter had disappeared. He hardly blamed Dick, and yet he was a little surprised. For, in days which Grant could remember, there was no man, and there was no danger on earth, on which Dick would have turned his back.

In the meantime, it behooved Grant to get out of Newbury at the first possible moment, for there was no doubt that the clever Dick Ware would soon be in touch with his enemies. He would make the report to the rest that Harry Grant had turned back on his trail and put his head in the lion's mouth.

The next thing, therefore, was to persuade Tommy to leave the town. But that was not easy. Perhaps the mere act of persuasion would have been a simple matter, but it was by no means easy to come within earshot of that youth. For all of the good men of Newbury were intent upon having him home with them to drink and dine.

A general compromise was effected. There was a celebration of the downfall of the bully, Morrissey, and the humiliation of his ally, Channing, by means of a large party in the hotel. And when Mr. Harry Grant finally got close to his young friend he found him engaged in an occupation which, of all others, commanded the religious respect of Mr. Grant. For he found Tommy at a table, playing poker with four men whose fat wallets disgorged money at every turn of the game.

The stack of chips before Tommy—who must have started the game with nothing—looked like the toy house of a child's building, so many little towers of red and blue chips were before him! Mr. Grant came to interrupt; he remained for a moment to admire reverently, with his intellectual hat removed, so to speak.

He saw Tommy working with dainty, deft fingers. He saw Tommy smiling and gay in victory and defeat. Having seen these things, he turned, went out from the room, and stepped onto the veranda of the hotel to let the cool of the evening wind touch his face. A light step approached him. He turned and saw, to his amazement, that none other than Dick Ware stood beside him.

It was very odd, odd, above all, that Dick cared to show himself in this town where he had been expected to stand and fight like a man that afternoon. But perhaps Dick was trusting to the shadows as a mask upon his face. That face was now wreathed with smiles of the most perfect content. There was such joy in his heart that it cast, as it were, a light before him. From that light, Mr. Grant shrank.

"Well, Dick?" he asked coldly. "What deviltry is in your head now? Or have you come back to Newbury to find out how popular you are in the town, now?"

"It's the one thing that I know already," answered Channing with a grin. "But I've come into town to tell you a thing *you* don't know, I take it."

"Are you sure?"

"Grant," said the other, "great a liar as you are, and cool as you are, still there's some way of touching you. And this is the news that I'm bringing you!"

Mr. Grant shifted, and his color altered. "It's about—" he began, and then paused.

"It's about Muriel," said the other. "You've guessed it right."

"A lie that the gang has made up for me, I suppose," said Grant.

"No, Harry. I ain't fool enough to think that I could pull the wool over your eyes. But I'll tell you the truth and the simple truth. She's cut and run with the Dean!"

19

Grant reached for the wall, found it, and leaned there, gasping.

"No—no," he whispered.

One could see something almost like pity in the face of Dick—but still there was more exultation than kindness in his eyes.

"She's gone where with him?" asked Grant.

"Is that part of the bargain—for me to tell you that?"

Harry Grant took him by the arm, and his hand was trembling. "Dick, I am a rich man—if I care to use my money."

"Money can't buy any news out of me, Harry. The lot of us wish you too far away. And if I blew the news to you and got a slice of your crooked money, how long would it last with me? The gang would tumble—and that would be the end of me. Don't beg me for news, Harry. I've done my share of talking. I've simply come to tell you that *you're* on the griddle, now, and it's our turn to sit back and laugh while we watch you dance!"

"Dick, did I ever harm a woman? It was men that I dealt with, always."

"*I* haven't done it to you," said Dick with a touch of shame. "It's the Dean's job. All his!"

"Tell me only when he got her away from her home."

"I'll tell you nothing."

"What difference will that make, Dick? If you only tell me when she left with him—was it a week ago—or yesterday—will it give me any clue to the *direction* they rode in, if you tell me only what day she left with him?"

"Harry, I know you too well. You start in thinking where I leave off and give up. You might find a way. And I'm not going to be the death of the Dean."

"A rat, Dick, who sticks a knife in a man's back!"

"A fair-and-square, stand-up fighter—the only one that ever stood up to you and beat you, fair and square. The gent that drove you into the high sticks and keeps you there because you don't dare to come out into the open and face him. Don't throw stones at the Dean."

Mr. Grant was too greatly tormented to resent these personal insults. He merely took the other arm of Dick Ware and pressed it with a trembling eagerness.

"If the Dean can beat me, then why not let me know where I can find him to fight it out with him?"

"Oh, I know that you'd fight for her."

"Dick, for heaven's sake!"

"Not a word out of me."

"You're a father yourself, Dick."

"Well, curse you, I'll tell you this much, and be hanged to you! It was this same day that he got her away from her home. But if you hunt a year and a day with a hundred men, you could never find the pair of them!"

Mr. Grant relaxed his grip from the arms of the other and stepped back. The night was thick in the valley where the town of Newbury lay, but still upon the distant peaks there was a faint light—or rather, a faint hint of a light. The day was not quite dead, and the same sun which had dropped behind those mountains had seen his daughter and the Dean leave his house.

He turned toward the door of the hotel; then, on second thought, he determined to get the horses ready first. So he went to the stable and saddled Dolly. But the black stallion acted like a black panther instead when Grant would have entered his stall.

Back to the hotel, he went to get Tommy. But before he had gone three strides from the stable door, there was a loud chorus of shouting from the building and then a rapid chattering of revolvers. An instant later, a lithe form leaped toward him and past him through the night.

"Start riding, Grant!" called the voice of Tommy as he raced past. "They're after me and they mean business."

"Turn Dolly loose. She'll come to me!" commanded Grant. "And I'll hold them back." The wind jerked a broad cloud in twain, emitting a flood of moonshine that showed to Grant half a dozen racing men—angry men—all plunging eagerly along the trail of Tommy. But as they charged out from the shadow of the trees, they were confronted by two long revolvers poised as in hands of stone by Mr. Grant.

All that they saw was a little man wearing a broad-brimmed hat which cast a black veil across his face; the revolvers were the main thing. They made the six come to a staggering halt, in their anxiety not to run into mortal danger.

"Stranger," panted one of them, "we've got the kid. We're bound to get him! There's twenty more coming behind us. Are you going to throw in with a ship that's about to sink?"

It sounded, from the confused shouting, as though half of the town were pouring toward them at that moment.

"What has he done?" asked Grant, edging closer to the shadow of a tree.

"Stacked the cards all evening. Cursed smart—and cursed crooked! He's got thirty thousand dollars in his pockets. And eight of the thirty belongs to me! Curse him if we don't paint him with tar and then add some feathers."

"Here he comes! Stranger, keep out of this—"

"Partners," said Harry Grant, "I've no doubt that you're

wise men. And if you want to prove it, you'll stay where you are. I'm bothered with bad nerves in both hands. If you budge, I'll plaster you with lead. I'll poultice you down with .45 slugs. So keep quiet!''

"They work the gag together!" groaned one of the six. "It's no use, Bill. They're in cahoots!"

Here was Dolly shaking her bridle at the side of her master. Yonder came Tommy on the black stallion, miraculously saddled in this instant of time!

"Take your horse," said Tommy calmly to his friend. "You, there—turn on your heels and let me see those guns drop when you turn. I'll like the looks of them on the ground. You understand?"

They turned with due precision. A wave from the hand of Tommy sent Harry Grant away into the night. He put the good mare at the rear fence that surrounded the hotel grounds—a good four and a half foot jump over strong boards. And as Dolly was scurrying through the dust of the street a block away, Grant heard the bang of guns and looked back in time to see the grand form of the stallion rising above the edge of the fence, like a winged thing against the stars.

Grant did not wait for his companion. He had seen Hagan's speed tested before, at the expense of his own pocketbook. Now he gave all of his attention to getting the best possible rate out of Dolly.

Even so, in five scant minutes—when the town was a dwindling row of lights behind them and the noise of a vague pursuit roared in the offing—the strong beating of hoofs drew up on Dolly's flank, and here was the black horse careening along with his head carried high, his ears pricking—as a horse canters when he is easily inside his strength and running for the pleasure of it—no more!

However, Dolly's own turn of speed had been enough. There was no danger from the men of Newbury on this night, at least! In another moment, jogging side by side, Harry Grant asked what folly or stupidity had enabled the four gamesters to tell what the nature of Mr. Tommy Mayo's luck might be.

"Before we had played one round," said Tommy, "I saw that I was with four crooks. I had only one bit of luck—they were all strangers. I didn't have to fight them in couples. But they did what they could. Only, Grant, when a crooked gamester plays with me his hand has to be *very* fast. Because, for the last few years, I've been sitting in front of a looking glass for at least an hour a day, and watching my own hands at work. Well, Grant, I've worked up enough speed to fool my own eyes even when I know what I'm looking for. But when some of those fellows who play rancher half the year—and crooked gambling the other half—try some of their thick-skinned tricks, it's like watching moving pictures of how a card trick should not be done!" He began to laugh.

"How did they nail you, Tommy?"

"They didn't nail me, really, by any fault of my own. But there was a fool who had been drinking moonshine. He was walking around the table watching the deal, and just as I was in the act of burying a card under the bottom of the pack, what should happen but this blockhead fell into my chair and unsteadied my hand. It wouldn't happen once in a thousand years.

"But I had been winning so big that the whole four of those rascals were watching me close and so they saw—more than they should have seen! The big chap in the brown coat, across the table from me, had the cash—and I hadn't turned my chips into money! When he saw that phony deal of mine he reached for his gun with his right hand, and for my jaw with his left. But I beat him to the punch.

"The table went down with a slam. The lamp banged on the floor, and somebody yelled that the house was on fire! A lucky thing, too, that the oil didn't catch. However, that yell paralyzed them. They started to bolt for the door—but they left the banker behind them, with me on top of him. I only needed five seconds to get what I wanted.

"Then I dived through the window. The next thing I knew,

I was legging it through the night and passing you on the jump. But all that saved the horse and the saddle for me, old-timer, was the fact that you were standing there in the nick of time. How the devil did you happen to be there so pat?"

"When young troops are fighting," said Mr. Grant, smiling through the darkness as he saw this chance of assuming a position of wisdom, "a good general always arranges to support them from the rear. I thought that the stakes were running a mite high when I looked in on the room a while ago."

"Grant, I'll never forget—"

"Nonsense! Never thank me! No more than I thanked you for nailing O'Neil for me. These things have to be done for one another by friends! I hear that you picked up around thirty thousand dollars."

"Not that much. My friend with the yellow whiskers put five thousand dollars in counterfeit money into the game!"

"Shoved that much queer, and those crooks—"

"I don't think they saw it. It happened when I had won so much that they were thinking of nothing but stopping me. I almost think that they may have hired the drunkard—"

"You think that they *may* have hired him? Son, are you as green as that? Of course he was working for one of them—or all of them! They wanted to break up the game. No matter whether they saw a thing or not, they would have pretended that they did! You're lucky to have your hide along with you without a hole in it—to say nothing of twenty-five thousand in hard cash!"

20

After that first moment of congratulation, Mr. Grant grew very silent. His heart was swelling with troubles of his own. At last, he said sharply:

"Are you tired, Tommy?"

"Fresh as a lark! I've made my first haul today!"

"May you have a hundred like it before they plant you under some cottonwood tree! If you're fresh, then let me tell you that we'll need everything that you have to give us before morning!"

"Fire away," said Tommy.

"There is one man in the world," said Mr. Grant, "whom I fear, Tommy! Heaven knows that I fear him as much as any schoolboy ever feared his master! I fear him so much, Tommy, that although you're a better fighter than almost any other man in the mountains—and although I still have a bit of an edge over you—still I'm afraid to tackle that man, afraid even for the two of us to tackle him!"

"Good!" said Tommy. "Then we won't do it until I'm in better practice."

"He's beyond guns," said Grant gloomily.

"Won't bullets hurt him?"

"He's been half blown to bits by 'em. And that's how he learned what he knows now. But we *are* going for him, Tommy. And we're going for him tonight."

Tommy whistled, but he made no spoken comment.

"How does it happen," asked Grant, at last, "that you know all about this town—and the two crooks who were in it—when not a one of them knew you?"

"Why," said Tommy, "I've spent a lot of time in these last years learning everything that I could about the mountains and the towns in the mountains. A fellow leading the sort of life that I plan to live, has to be a good deal of a student. I've studied hard, Grant!" And he began to laugh softly to himself.

"You've mapped the country in your head?" snapped Grant.

"Every inch of it. I've sneaked away on trips. They used to fight to keep me at work on the ranch. But after a while even dad's wife was sort of glad to see me go. After that, I used to cruise around and find what I could find. There's always *something* to find in the mountains, Grant! I've mapped every stream. I know where the trout are. I know where the game is. I know where to hunt with a gun and where to hunt with a trap. I've even marked out the home sections of the three big grizzlies that live in our section. All of that stuff is worth knowing when a man gets into a pinch.

"I've found out about the towns and all the people in the towns, as far as I could remember them. I've learned the names and tried to get the pictures of the big ranchers and bankers and the folks with the ready coin. Besides that, I have a list of the sheriffs and their best deputies, and all the hard-riding, straight-looking men that I can hear about. You hear about a rogue's gallery. Well, I keep one with pictures of the other kind. Those four fellows in Newbury were all new to me—names and faces. So I knew they were strangers. And that was one of the many reasons that I wanted to trim them!"

Mr. Grant listened to this recital of strange studies with the greatest interest, nodding his head from time to time.

"Tell me now," said he, "if you know the lay of the land as far as to Great Gloster Mountain?"

"I know it that far like a book."

"Punch that point down in your mind and make it the center for a compass to swing from. Now, with that point for a beginning, go over the mountains with your mind. Don't draw a narrow compass. Open it out to forty miles. Can you go that far to the north?"

"Yes."

"And every other direction?"

"Yes."

"About thirty-five to forty-five miles from Great Gloster Mountain, is there a minister's house, anywhere in that circle that you're drawing?"

Tommy closed his eyes and gave himself up to patient thought.

"Thirty miles north—there's a town—"

"Not a town, if possible!"

"A minister's house not in a town?"

"If that's possible?"

"A minister's house not in a town," murmured the youth to himself. "But there's only one of those that I know anything about. That's about—"

"How far from Gloster Mountain?"

"Nearly fifty miles, I guess. Thirty miles from here."

Grant groaned.

"Are you that much set on getting at this fellow?" asked Tommy with much surprise, and even with a trace of sympathy.

"I've got to find him," said Grant. "I've got to reach him, no matter what happens when the showdown comes! But fifty miles is too far. They wouldn't ride over such a stretch. What direction from Gloster Mountain?"

"West."

"West!" echoed Grant gloomily. "And that would be the

direction toward his own home country! Tommy, I'm afraid that that's the place! How far from here?"

"Thirty miles."

"Thirty miles—thirty devils!"

He jerked out his cigar case, but instead of lighting his smoke, he merely chewed savagely at the tobacco, groaning in his anguish.

"Well," he said at last, "you're not mistaken? You know the minister, do you?"

"I know all about him. Everything. He's the minister who rode with the gang that hunted down the band of rustlers who robbed the Lewis outfit of fifteen hundred head and tried to shoot them across the river and over the line. His name is Derby. He's fifty years old, rides like an Indian, shoots as well as anyone, and lives all by himself in the mountains.

"He put up a shack at a sort of a cross trail—and there he spends his life. When people come along he gives them chuck and, if he gets a chance, he reads a bit of the Bible to them. On Sundays, he rings a big bell that he's got. He rings it early in the morning and in the middle of the morning. The punchers, when they hear that noise floating over the hills, come sliding down to see him.

"They're not ashamed to go to the Derby church. There's no singing, no organ, no church steeple, no hardwood benches, no passing of the plate, no all-fired long sermon. But old Derby just sits down with the rest and reads to 'em out of the Bible and talks to 'em. He's that kind. And if—"

"Curse the rest of it," exclaimed Mr. Harry Grant. "Do I care what he is? You'll be quoting some of the stuff he reads to them, before long. You know Derby, and that's enough for me. He's fifty years old. He's a rough one."

"He's as smooth as silk," said Tommy. "I've looked up a lot of the stories about him."

"Never mind," snapped Grant. "I don't care what the stories were about. What I want to do is to reach that sky pilot and reach him fast. Is there a shortcut through those hills—something that will whittle away part of the distance?"

"No."

"There must be!" He added, after a moment of impatient writhing in the saddle: "I'll give you light while you draw a plan of the trail. Then I'll see for myself if there's a cut-off."

Tommy obediently dismounted and, while Grant lighted one match after another, Tommy smoothed down a bit of sand and traced the trail on it swiftly—as swiftly as though he had a map to which to refer.

"Here's a creek. We have to go two miles east to get to a ford. Then we climb hills—steep ones, too. When we get to the crest of 'em we swing to the left—here. There's the old burned-down Justis place on the right and there's the remains of what was once a good road."

"Can't you shorthand this description?"

"As fast as you want it. We keep swinging to the left for three more miles, after that, and then we bear straight ahead for nine more, at the end. There's the house of Derby chucked down at the cross trail."

He drilled a hole in the sand with a slender forefinger.

"Very well," said Mr. Grant. "You've planned a nice little circular ride for us. Why shouldn't we cut across the arc of the circle? We would save a good half of the distance."

"No," said Tommy Mayo, "we don't ride that way."

"Why not?"

"It's one tangle of trouble from the start. You can't go that way even by day. And by night—I wouldn't tackle it even with Hagan—and your mare would break a leg or tumble you down a cliff before you had gone three miles!"

"Tommy," said the older man, laying a tense hand upon the shoulder of his companion, "we're going to ride the shortcut. We can't waste that time. It isn't *all* rough going."

"Four miles, I suppose."

"Why, boy, we could almost *jump* that far!"

"You're a dead man, Grant, if you go that way!"

"One of us will get through."

"What good is one of us to do this job?"

"What do you mean?"

"You told me that the Dean was too much for you."

"Any time other than tonight. Tonight I'm a match for him, Tommy, if you will take the chance with me."

"I'll go along with you until you break the horse's neck or your own," said Tommy. "Then I'll pick up the pieces and come back."

"Show the way!"

"This way," called Tommy, and led off to the left.

In an instant they were climbing with labor up a steep slope.

"What's wrong?" called Tommy, seeing the saddle of his companion empty all at once.

"I can save her strength by running up the hill. She may need all that she has before she's through!"

"She'll need it, well enough. Now watch yourself! Because here's where the trouble begins!"

21

As he spoke, the horses stopped of their own accord. They had come to the ridge which formed one wall of a ravine. Out of the darkness beneath them rose the scent of pines. Grant, straining his eyes, tried to make out the tangle.

"It's all thicket." He sighed.

"All the way across," said Tommy. "Your clothes will be rags before you get to the other side."

"Curse the clothes. But how steep is it?"

"See for yourself. No, I'll show you the way."

The black stallion dipped over the edge of the valley wall and seemed to plunge straight down toward destruction. He did not walk but slid out of sight. Presently he could be heard crashing through the shrubbery beneath.

Now there was silence, and then to the anxious ear of Mr. Grant came a faint halloo.

"Safe? Bear to the right of the slide I made. I was nearly wrecked on a rock!"

Mr. Grant sent Dolly at the black descent. She, good horse as she was, balked for a moment. It was, indeed, very much like suicide. Presently he half soothed and half threatened her into the attempt. Once over the edge, there was no question of delay or second thought. Poor Dolly was struggling to save her life as they rushed down through lashing boughs and reaching, entangling vines that caught viciously at the flying hoofs.

They came with a sudden, staggering shock to the bottom of the gulch. There was the black and his rider, waiting.

"Is there much more like that?" gasped Grant.

"That's merely the beginning. Do you want to keep on?"

"Four miles of this going?"

"Worse than this—up and down!"

"It's not possible!"

"I've heard about this country—every inch. Sam Douglas used it when he was dodging the law. He kept away from the hangman for four years by living here in the gulches. It's worse than this a bit farther. No trees, even—just rocks!"

The thought of Grant was not for himself. "Will the mare stand it?" he groaned.

"You'll kill her," said Tommy calmly.

"She'll never die in a better cause."

"You'll go on?"

"Yes, heaven help me! Will you stick with me, son?"

"I'll stay as long as the mare stays. Here we go!"

They threaded their way through a heavy growth of trees at the bottom of the ravine, and almost instantly the climb of the farther wall began. It was the reverse of the descent. They had to dismount and blindly fumble among the shrubbery for hand holds while they dragged themselves up and up, leading the horses by the reins.

Once the stallion found loose footing and slid back fifty feet before he could stop his impetus. But he came fighting back, and presently they were at the crest of the rise again. Half a mile of steady climbing followed. They kept the horses at a steady trot. The black horse went through the rocks as though the broadest day were shining; but not so Dolly.

She did her best, and a very gallant best it was. But she lacked that extra sense with which the stallion was equipped. She had never been schooled in the great outdoors, fighting for her living through winter and summer, and learning to hunt for the most inaccessible rocks of the mountains when the men came whirling in pursuit after her.

From this school Hagan had gone and graduated with honors. He had a way to sense an obstruction before it loomed on him through the night, and his hoofs went daintily among the rocks. Poor Dolly was floundering constantly. Twice she was down—up again instantly, but with nerves shaken, strength leaving her, surety used up.

They had struggled across the second ridge and gone down the slope of the third canyon when, in the rush through the level bottomland, Dolly went down with a crash. Tommy went back and untangled Grant from the struggling, kicking horse. The man was limp and totally out for a moment, but he recovered quickly enough. His concern was for the mare. But as he started toward her, Dolly came gallantly to her feet.

"Good girl!" cried Grant. "I thought I had spoiled her that time, Tommy! I don't know what she tripped on."

"You may have spoiled her, after all," suggested Tommy. "She's lamed in front."

"You lie, Tommy!" cried Grant. "I'd rather lose half a million than be without a horse tonight."

Tommy laughed faintly in the darkness. "I don't know about the half million," he said, "but you're as good as without a horse. The only thing Dolly can do for you now is to keep you company. Shall we build a fire here?"

Grant did not reply to these cool remarks. He was leading the mare up and down. There was no doubt about it—she was lamed and badly lamed. Perhaps she was ruined forever!

But what mattered to Grant was the loss of a means of crossing those mountains and the ten long miles beyond them.

"Tommy," he said suddenly, "you're going on with this job for me, tonight!"

Tommy merely laughed again.

"I say you are!" cried Grant.

"There's no good in talk. I told you what I'd do. I'd go as far as you'd go, tonight. But no farther."

"Are you a coward?" snarled Grant venomously.

"You can't insult me," said Tommy with perfect poise, "so long as there's no one else to hear you. But don't bother me too much."

"Will you let me take the horse from you, Tommy?"

"Let you? If you can stick on his back, you're welcome."

Grant groaned and struck his hands against his forehead.

"I'm done for!" said he.

"Look here," said Tommy. "What's so bad about it?"

"The Dean—a devil, not a man."

"If he's such a fighter, he can't be such a bad sort of a fellow."

"You don't know him. If you did, Tommy, you'd be tearing away on to the mountains."

"Not I! A man who's too hard for you to tackle alone, is too hard for me."

"Boy—fool! I've seen you fight! I've watched your gun play. Tommy, don't you understand that there's not a man in the mountains that you need to be afraid of?"

"Thanks," said Tommy. "I'd like to think that, too. But I'm taking no chances."

"The whole happiness of a girl, Tommy!"

"The devil!" said Tommy with a sudden disgust. "What are women to me? I'd rather take the chance for the sake of a man. But a girl? Grant, I'm sorry for you—but that's all you get out of me."

Mr. Grant did not reply, at once. He threw away the tattered remnants of his cigar and lighted another from the inexhaustible case in his coat pocket. While the burning spot glowed at the end of the cigar, he sat down on a fallen tree in the heart of the ravine.

"Good," said Tommy. "That smoke ought to keep off mosquitoes."

He paid no further attention to his companion except to say: "I'm ready to start on, whenever you give the word."

Then he brought out his flute, screwed it together, and presently he was whistling a tune on it, so faint and small that it did not disturb the thoughts of Mr. Grant. Rather, it ran smoothly in with the current of his reflections, until he stood up with a gasp.

Grant sat down again and drew from his pocket the eternal cigar case, but this time it was not for the purpose of touching the contents. He merely turned back the morocco flap and on the inside of it, when he lighted a match, there showed the photograph of a girl.

Mr. Grant stared at this for a long time until he became aware that something had altered in the scene. It was the whistling of Tommy which had ceased. Now he turned and by the last flicker of the match he saw that Tommy was regarding the picture with much concern.

"She's not a winner for beauty, eh?" remarked Tommy.

"There's no man on earth good enough to have her," said Mr. Grant with a sad conviction. "But I'm beaten—and she's lost. Let's build a fire here. Have you a scrap of paper in your pocket?"

In place of answering, Tommy said: "She has a clean look, though—a very clean look! She reminds me of a good-blooded colt. I like the cut of her face, Grant."

Mr. Grant had had some difficulty in coming to understand his new friend, but in the process of time he had come to learn that it was better to let Tommy fumble toward things and decisions in his own way, because he could not be hurried. Therefore, Mr. Grant sat still—and said not a word— but held his breath. He would not break the lucky spell even to brush from his face the dozen of mosquitoes which landed there and began to sting him.

Tommy stirred again and sighed. "What manner of a looking man is this Dean?" he asked.

"Dean Thomas," said Grant, "is a queer-looking fellow, with sandy eyebrows and sandy eyes! He is an inch or two over six feet. He looks as if he weighs a hundred and sixty pounds. He's twenty pounds heavier. He looks as if he were about to fall asleep, half the time. But he never closes an eye. He looks as though he were a good-natured, lazy fellow. But he's a cruel devil, and his wits are never still. Curse him and double curse him! Killing me was not enough for him. He had to hurt me in a nearer way than that. And so he has my girl!''

"You and the Dean are real partners," Tommy chuckled.

"Tommy, there was a time when he and I worked together in the same gang. I'll tell you this much. It may be worth your knowing. It was the Dean that persuaded me to double-cross the gang. He robbed me of the profits and left me with the blame.''

"If he has your scalp, why is he after you now?"

"He hates me because he has injured me, Tommy. He hates me because he knows that he's the only man in the world that I fear. Those are his reasons. He knew that he could run me down—no man can keep away from the Dean! He could run me down and finish me. But three years ago he told me that he was laying his plans and that they would be ripe in three more years. He meant that he was waiting for my girl to grow old enough for marriage. And now he has her.''

"You told her about him?"

"Does a man tell his children about the devil? Of course I told her!''

"She doesn't *look* like a fool," said Tommy thoughtfully.

"Young man, she's a long, long distance from that! Trust me that she is a long distance from that! But what do lessons matter when a girl sees a handsome man? And the Dean can be as gentle as running water!''

"I see," murmured Tommy.

He whistled, and the black stallion glided up to him and stood at wait, with the starlight glimmering on his sweat-burnished flanks. Tommy rubbed Hagan's velvet muzzle.

"I think Hagan can get me there," said he. "But cursed if I know what will happen, after I arrive. I don't suppose that it will do any good for me to tell her that you're not happy to have her marry the Dean?''

"No good in the world! I don't know what you can do, either. Your own wits will tell you after you arrive there. You have one chance. One in a hundred, Tommy. Are you going to take it?''

Tommy, in place of answering, swung himself into the saddle.

"If you strike out on foot," he said, "you might be able to get there in time to do some good. Or at least you could shoot the skunk before he's buried me. So long!''

He did not pause to receive thanks, but he swung away at once on the stallion. Two of the long strides of Hagan carried him out of sight into the black of the night.

22

Grant did not follow on the same trail at once. In fact, he merely remained standing and staring and listening to faint noises on the farther wall of that ravine until, at length, a dislodged rock far up the side rolled down and started larger stones. These in turn dislodged a shower of boulders that stormed down to the floor of the valley, crashing among the trees. A great rock fragment rebounding from the valley floor came significantly close to the head of Mr. Grant, with a sinister, whirring noise.

He listened, with his heart stopped, until the last roaring echo had died away. Then he shouted. There was no reply! And yet surely young Tommy had not ridden out of earshot, and clear over the edge of the valley, in this short time. It seemed to mean only one thing—that the noisy shower of ruin which had just smashed down into the gulch had carried with it the bodies of glorious Hagan and Tommy Mayo!

Mr. Grant thought of that, but the next moment he forgot horse and man and remembered that the last hope had been stripped from him of saving his daughter.

Just then, as despair was taking him firmly by the throat, he heard, far off and faintly on the wind, the trill of a whistled tune—only a fragment of an air. It was enough to make Harry Grant throw up his arms foolishly into the night and then start forward at a stumbling run to follow on the same trail with all his might.

He had not much hope of arriving at the place in time to be of any help in whatever need might arise—but he went because he could not remain there alone and inactive in the wilderness while young Tommy rushed ahead to fight the great battle.

Hope and terror poured through Mr. Grant alternately. Sometimes he thought of the flaccid youth who had yawned at the house of Jack Mayo—and then it seemed that it was like flinging a handful of roses into the face of a giant to oppose the terrible Dean with this boy.

Again, he remembered how Tommy had walked into Newbury with Hagan behind him, hunting men, and finding them. And he remembered how the warning cry had come from behind— and how that savage miscreant, Morrissey, had fired with a sure aim—and how he had fallen under the boy's fire.

Most of all, he recalled that manner of Tommy's—standing calmly watching as he saw Morrissey with murderous determination try to fire another shot. That was the true test of steel, and it seemed to Grant that there was in the boy the stuff that may bend but which will not break. To be sure, the Dean was a dreadful fighter—and yet a sort of superstitious sense of luck in Tommy made Grant keep a hope of success for him.

Having launched a career of rascality with so much fervor, it did not seem possible that any man's hand could arrest the progress of the boy. For the devil would see to that! What ridiculous economy if he claimed his own before Tommy Mayo had tumbled at least half a dozen souls to the devil!

So reasoned Mr. Grant, or rather, so he talked to himself as he struggled forward through that wild night—avoiding reason— clinging to superstitions, and sometimes almost praying, lifting his face to the black sky and to the rain.

For it was raining now. The wind had been rising for some

time, and now it carried stinging volleys of water. Grant, clambering up slippery rocks, or sliding down drenched slopes, wondered with all his heart how a horse could ever have managed that trail. Even in the hearts of the valleys, besides, there were frequent down scoopings of the wind, and on the high ridges between the hollows, a gale tore at him.

Yet Grant felt an odd certainty that the youngster was still forging ahead through that wild night. He himself was tattered, battered and bruised, his wind gone, his shoes split. What was the condition of the great horse and the young rider?

The horse and rider were already coming to the end of the bitter four-mile journey through the mountains. Though Tommy was not of a type addicted to wonder, he could not but marvel, now, at the unflagging power with which Hagan sped on through the night. There was not the blind and headlong fury with which even the best and most generous horse attacks a great work. Rather there was a sort of feline cunning about Hagan.

He judged his work before he did it. A dozen times he would falter on the brink of a descent before he found, or sensed through the dark, the proper point at which to make the effort. But, once embarked, he went crashing down to the bottom of the gulch!

The last rise was topped. And with the easier country spreading beneath him, young Tommy paused and dismounted. He was drenched with rain. His coat was a mass of soaked tatters, flapping in the gale. He was covered with cuts and scratches; he ached in a thousand points where heavy limbs of trees had smitten him in passing. His fine sombrero was gone, long ago, and every drop of the wind-driven rain beat through his hair to the skull with a stinging force.

However, his concern was not, at that moment, for himself. He passed his hands carefully over each inch of the body of Hagan, until he made sure that all was well with the big black. That done, he looked to the cinches. The tremendous work across the rough country had tucked up the big animal a little and the girths needed tightening. After that, Tommy was in the saddle again, trotting Hagan down the slope toward the long and level road beneath.

For that was typical of Tommy. Now that he had a down slope and the rough work ended, he went at it most leisurely; his haste was all left behind him and he considered, systematically, in what manner he could get the greatest speed for the greatest number of miles out of Hagan.

It would not be by rushing him downhill and staving in his forelegs by such heavy pounding! Therefore, not until they reached the level, did he give Hagan a bit more urging. For the horse was like his master—not overeager, not pressing on the bit, but quietly ready for whatever might come.

There was a sudden falling off in the strength of the rainfall, also. It dropped to a mere mist. Underfoot there was good, firm sand which the rain had not reduced to pulp but merely beaten harder. On this congenial footing, Hagan flew along—eleven miles, but all stretched smooth, or merely rolling easily among gentle hills. Who could have asked for better going? Not Hagan! The miles dropped quickly behind him.

They came, at last, to a steep lifting in the trail, and when Hagan had jogged to the top of it, his master saw, not a quarter of a mile away, two dim yellow eyes looking toward him, the rays of light splitting the finest spangles as they passed through the showering rain. There was the house of the minister.

Someone had called him the apostle of the mountains, and even Tommy, in his strange heart, admitted a slight feeling of awe, perhaps; though who could say what actually passed in the heart of Tommy Mayo? He let the stallion go on at a jogging pace, and as he rode he worked steadily at his wrists and hands, bringing the blood back into the chilled, numbed flesh. For he would need supple, accurate fingers before the night was ended.

When he got to the house he rode ruthlessly across the little garden in front of the cabin. He peered through the window and saw that the interior was empty except for the "apostle" himself. He sat near the open fire on the farther side of the rough chamber, and only a bit of his iron-gray hair and his burly shoulder and his crossed legs were visible, ensconced as he was in the depths of the easy chair.

Tommy was out of the saddle instantly and knocking at the door.

"Hello? Come in!"

He stepped in and stood for a moment in the shadow close to the door. So it was that the Reverend Nicholas Derby had his first glimpse of the youth—his first of many sights of him. He has stated that his first sense was a chilling one of fear; he goes even further, declaring that, with the opening of the door, even before he laid eyes upon Tommy, an uncanny thrill went swiftly through his flesh.

But, as someone has remarked, it was a damp night, and the open door let in a draft! However, one was inclined to take the clergyman seriously, because he was not an oversensitive man. He was as broad and bulky and leather skinned as any cowpuncher that ever rode the range. However, when Tommy actually came into the room—then there was reason for a bit of apprehension on the part of Mr. Derby, for Tommy remained a long moment in the shade by the door.

He did so because there was a big double burner on the table in the middle of the room, and Tommy did not wish to step forward until his eyes were a little accustomed to the light. Mr. Derby had to exclaim: "Come out and show yourself, man!"

Then Tommy stepped forward, and Nicholas Derby was fond of describing the picture that he saw in that moment. What he found first of all, of course, was simply a ragged, storm-swept waif, cast into his house and offered to his charity by the rigors of the night. He started up.

"What the devil has happened to you?" said the Reverend Nicholas, part of whose vocabulary was most unclerical. "Who has been beating you about—or have you been playing tag with a mountain lion?"

"I stubbed my toe," said Tommy, "and I fell into a bramble bush. Thanks for the makings. Mine are a little damp."

This he said as he stepped to the mantelpiece above the fire, taking brown papers and tobacco which he found there. He had to dry his hands before he could handle the papers without crumbling them. While he rolled his smoke he looked down upon Mr. Derby with a smile which, Derby declares, was rather in his brown eyes than upon his lips.

"Help yourself," said the minister.

And he busily took stock of his visitor. He decided that his age was in the early twenties—or was he five years older? He was about five feet and nine inches—or was he actually six feet? He might weigh a hundred and fifty pounds, by the lightness of his step—or a hundred and seventy, when one regarded more closely the thickness of his neck and that depth of chest which means so much.

But above all, Mr. Derby knew that his guest was either a vagabond or a gentleman; he could tell it by the softness and taper delicacy of the fingers of Tommy Mayo.

"Young man," said he, "what are you doing on such a night? I almost believe—that you've ridden the shortcut!"

"I have," said Tommy and closed his eyes while he inhaled a deep breath of tobacco smoke.

23

The reason that the minister stared so very much was that he himself had made the crossing of the shortcut. But he had made it many years before, when his strength was on him and all his supple vigor of youth. He had made it on the back, not of a horse, but of a very well-trained mule. Yet, it had been an experience such as he had never forgotten. It went down as the most trying physical experience of his life. And he considered what the storm must have been in the mountains.

Actually he had mentioned the shortcut as a sort of very extravagant metaphor. And here was a daring young man who presumed to say that he had actually gone through that inferno of battling winds and raging rain and slippery rocks, and tearing brush and cliffs and thickets.

"Well, young fellow," said the minister, "you look almost bad enough for me to believe you!"

Tommy, with his eyes closed inhaling that breath of smoke, had seemed a mere child. Now, as he opened them again, he seemed many years older. He held his cigarette poised, as though he were about to speak. But he did not speak. There was no sound but the dripping of the water from his clothes for a long moment. But it seemed to the Reverend Nicholas that a dim yellow light was gathering in the brown eyes of the young stranger; a will-o'-the-wisp hint of a yellow light, and that was all. It was enough to make Derby stiffen in his chair.

"I don't mean to call you a liar," he said. "But there are not half a dozen men who have ridden the shortcut even by day!"

"I know!" said Tommy. "A place gets a reputation like that, and then people are afraid."

He had finished the cigarette, and tossed the butt into the fire. The smoke was still streaming from his nostrils.

"What's your name?" asked Derby.

"Mayo. Tommy Mayo."

Mr. Derby had heard that name a number of times very recently. He had heard it on this very evening, for he had built—chiefly by his own labor—five miles of telephone wire, climbing the nearest ridge and dropping to the tiny village beyond it. That village was connected by wire with Newbury, and Newbury stretched out electric fingers to the brain and heart of the world.

Not all the news came to him, but through it there seeped such items as were most likely to appeal to Western minds. When these items reached the next village there was sure to be someone who remembered the lonely house of the preacher. Hence there were long conversations on nearly every evening. But tonight there had been only one major article of news.

Newbury had been stood upon its head; the terrible Morrissey, beaten in fair fight, lay desperately wounded—nearly dying of shame and rage, the pockets of four strangers, four prosperous visitors to the town, had been emptied, so they said, of thirty thousand dollars. News like this, to be sure, *was* worth repetition. But what staggered the minister was the calm with which the boy asserted his name.

"Tommy Mayo!" he echoed. "Well, my son, I suppose you think that the news comes slowly up this way. But sometimes it comes fast enough. I have a telephone and I've been listening to stories about the shooting of Morrissey."

"Yes?"

"And how four strangers were cheated out of thirty thousand dollars in a poker game?"

"It was only twenty-five thousand," said Tommy. "Five thousand dollars was counterfeit stuff."

Mr. Derby gasped again. "A lucky day for you then," said he with much hidden irony.

"Fairly lucky," said Tommy. And he began to roll another cigarette.

"My dear young friend," said the minister with a sudden burst of unction, "I wish—"

Tommy stopped him with a raised hand. "Don't say it," said he. "Don't say it. It'll do no good. But if you start with advice, it will spoil a pleasant time for us. The way it is, we ought to know each other. You're the honest man, and I'm the crook. The pair of us ought to do very well together!"

"That's an original idea," said Derby. "I suppose that you have led a pretty easy life, Tommy?"

"Easy in a way," said Tommy thoughtfully; "but hard in a way. I've been waiting and working for years, now, to get ready for the time when I could be free to tackle a crook's life. It takes a lot of training, you know!"

"I'd never thought of it in that way," said the preacher.

"I supposed that you haven't. But suppose I put it like this: It's easy for me to get five dollars from you by working a day. But is it easy for me to steal five dollars out of your purse? When I try to steal your purse you reach for a gun. If you miss, you send for the law. And it's a hard thing to beat the law!"

"Is it ever worthwhile?" asked Derby.

"What else is left, if a fellow wants a little fun?" asked the sober gambler. "What else can you do, except play tag with the law? Or else try a game like yours. Up here, all by yourself, with nobody near, it isn't so bad to be a minister. But I suppose that you'd rather be a crook like me than to be a minister down in the city where there are a thousand other preachers, just like you!"

Mr. Derby started to answer in haste, and then he observed

that Tommy Mayo had spoken rather in the tone of one who discusses than one who argues with heat. So he changed his mind, hunted for an answer of the same sort, and, for the first time in many years, felt a twinge of discontent with his soul dart through him.

He was a brave and honest man, however, and that admission was wrung from him: "I suppose that there is something in what you say, young man. I'm up here in the mountains partly because it's spectacular. It makes people talk about me."

"Yes," said Tommy. "That's one of the reasons. It's exciting. But I'm not the kind that wants that sort of excitement. Being good isn't attractive to me, I suppose—unless there were some sort of gambling chance connected with it. If the devil were around in these days putting up bids, it might be more fun to play against him; but he hasn't been showing up for a few centuries except in print. And there he's a bore."

Mr. Derby was so fascinated that he could merely stare at his visitor. "Will you tell me, Tommy Mayo," said he at last, "why it is that you choose to come in here and tell me all of these unpleasant things about yourself?"

"Are they unpleasant? I thought they were rather interesting."

"Of course, they are. But what will they make me think is in your mind?"

"You'll only remember that everybody needs to confess once in a while. Besides, I've got to make you trust me, tonight."

"Make me trust you! And so you begin by confessing that you have been shooting men and stealing money this very day?"

"A fair fight," said Tommy. "And the money was won, not stolen. They were all crooks. How many honest ranchers go around with thirty thousand in cash to *lose*!"

"That's true. However—you ran for it, Tommy, you know! And that doesn't look any too well!"

"It was a great mistake," said Tommy, nodding. "I should have stuck it out, and while the lights were out, I should have tackled the four of them with all my might—a gun or a knife or both. I might have laid out the whole quartet. Anyway, if I had remained, people would never have believed that a crook had stayed to fight it out. Honest men are supposed to stay and fight, but thieves run away."

He yawned lazily and stretched his body with a deep groan of comfort. "I have to remember that against the next time."

"And you tell me all this for the pleasure of confession— and to make me trust you? Trust you with what, Tommy?"

"With some information. I tell you frankly that I've been a crook today, so that you will be able to believe me when I tell you that I intend to be an honest man tonight!"

"Good!" said the minister. "What is it that you want to know, young Tommy Mayo?"

"In the first place—how many were there in the party?"

"What party?"

"The wedding party?"

"What do you know about that?"

"Not as much as I want to know."

"What do you wish me to tell you?"

"The number with Dean Thomas and the girl."

"Why?"

"I want to follow them. If there are too many of—"

"There are half a dozen with him, young man."

"Not that many! Is it two, or three?"

"How can you tell that there are not that many?"

"By the puddles of water on the floor. But most by the prints of the feet, you know. I know that there were two or three men with him. Two, I hope."

"Two," admitted the minister. "What else do you want to know?"

"How long ago were they here?"

"What will you do with this information?"

"Follow them, when you tell me the direction they rode in."

"They are all freshly mounted. They cleaned out my barn of all the good horseflesh in it, and they went storming along like a whirlwind, you see. You could never overtake them with an animal that had crossed the mountains!''

"I have Hagan," said the boy. "You have to remember that!"

"Hagan!" murmured Mr. Derby. "That's right. And what is the purpose of following them?"

"To give a message to the girl."

"From whom?"

"Her father."

"Will you tell me who that is?"

"A friend of mine. I left him halfway across the shortcut when his horse played out."

"Tommy, I begin to feel that I almost *ought* to tell you."

"You ought to. Do you know Dean Thomas?"

"You mean that he has been a bad actor? But he's over that. He's an honest man today, Tommy!"

"A smart man to make you think that he's honest! That's all. Only smart."

"But if he's really the terror that he used to be, what do you or any other man mean by riding after him?"

"I'm ready to take my chance. That's all! It's a gain for you honest people, no matter how it turns out. When we tangle, one crook dies—and that's an end to it!"

He added: "Perhaps both of us might go down!"

Mr. Derby stood up. "I'll do this for you, gladly," said he. "I'll put you up for the night, feed you, give you a dry set of clothes in the morning, and start you on your way. But as for information of any kind about any other people—except the dead—I can't open my mouth about it."

"Am I as bad as that?"

"You are too clever for me," said the minister. "You could pull the wool over my eyes too easily. And I don't want to run the risk of giving you that chance. Will you turn in and have a long sleep?"

"I'll have a piece of bread and a cup of coffee," said Tommy. "Haven't you a cook in the kitchen?"

"I have for this month. I'll take you out to him—"

"Never mind," said Tommy and stepped suddenly through the door and into the fragrance of a country kitchen where the odors of a whole store were crowding in the moist air.

"Mr. Derby," said he to a withered old man who was hobbling around from stove to sink, "says that you saw Dean Thomas and the wedding party after he did. What direction were they riding in?"

"Why, north of—"

But here the minister himself burst in on them with a shout. It had occurred to him, too late, that his guest might enter the kitchen for something other than food.

"Have you told him anything?" he asked the old man.

"Only that the weddin' party was riding toward Kensington."

"You've said enough and too much!" groaned Mr. Derby. "Confound your wagging tongue!"

24

But Tommy Mayo merely laughed. He laughed at the old man and he laughed at Mr. Derby, while he helped himself to a hot cup of coffee from the great pot which, night and day, simmered on the back of the stove and filled the house with hospitable perfumes. He swallowed a crust of bread, washed it down with the steaming coffee and then he went back into the other room with gloomy Derby.

"I shall ride with you," said Derby. "I *shall* ride with you, Tommy Mayo."

"You could never keep up with Hagan," declared the boy. "Give up that hope, I advise you. Good night. Why wouldn't the lot of them stay here, for the night?"

"All of them wanted to, except Dean Thomas. But he seemed to suspect that there would be a pursuit. Does he know you and your nature, young man?"

"He has never heard of me. He'll meet me for the first time tonight."

"Adios, then, Tommy." "Adios."

So Tommy left the house and hurried out into the rain and to Hagan. He found the black stallion standing in the lee of the house, already warm and steaming and contentedly dining off the luscious trailers of the climbing vine which wound up the side of the house. Then, in the saddle once more, but wonderfully warmed and strengthened by food and drink— with Hagan almost equally refreshed beneath him—he started on the trail.

He did not ride far, however. Not two miles from the house of Mr. Derby, Tommy drew rein again and put Hagan under the shelter of a grove of pines. It was hardly a shelter, for he did not penetrate deeply enough among the trees to be shielded from the sweep of the wind and the rain, and there was a steady, dreary dripping from the foliage above them. It was the trail that Tommy watched from this uncomfortable point of vantage. Presently, he was rewarded by seeing, down that trail, the advance of a sweeping shadow. It came closer; now it resolved itself in a horse, crashing through the storm with a rider with head downward to the rush of wind and of rain. Tommy did not wait to make inquiries. In such a time as this, the first thought would have to serve as the last thought, also.

He put the spurs to Hagan. It was the first time that the august flanks of that gallant horse had ever felt steel and he responded by trying to leap out of his skin. In an instant they were beside the other rider and the muzzle of Tommy's revolver rested in the small of the stranger's back.

"Pull up!" said Tommy.

The other obeyed at once, and the calm, deep voice of Mr. Derby sounded through the night. "What do you want? Why, Tommy Mayo, you've made a mistake this time, my boy. I'm Derby!"

"I know you," said Tommy. "Get off the horse."

"Now, what do you—"

"Get off the horse," cried Tommy in an apparent passion. "Am I to have you sneaking along behind me all the night?"

When wise men hear such a tone as that in which Tommy addressed his recent benefactor, they do not hesitate. They do as they are ordered and they do it quickly. Mr. Derby was a wise man. He dismounted from his horse and allowed Tommy to take the reins, making no protest, whatever.

Only he said, at the last: "In the old days I used to carry guns, Tommy!"

"In the old days," said Tommy, "you used to be a man!"

And he rode off with the captured horse.

As for Mr. Derby, he was not angered so much as he was saddened, and he was saddened not only by what had been done to him by Tommy Mayo as by what Tommy had said in departing. At any rate, all chance of catching up with Tommy, or even of following so closely that he might arrive at the scene to prevent a disaster, passed from the mind of the good man. And he merely said to himself that he had done his best. A poor consolation!

After all, he felt that there was a stinging scruple of truth in the thing that Tommy had said to him. In the old days, after all, he might have been a better man than he was now—a less charitable man, perhaps, but a man more respected for his strength—a less generous man, perhaps, but one capable of more charities because his labors had given him a greater income to dispense among the poor and the needy.

It was a sad and slow walk that Mr. Derby pursued to the house at the crossroads. There he sat by the fire telling himself that Tommy, after all, could never find, except by miracle, the place where, he was sure, the party of Dean Thomas would have sought shelter for the night. And now, as Derby sat by the fire, he began to tell himself that the old content which had so filled him would never be his again, as long as he lived.

This gay young man, flaunting his crookedness and his frankness before the eyes of the world, had simply stripped away the outer fortifications of the soul of the minister and left exposed the truth about himself.

What that truth was, Mr. Derby did not care to linger over. He lay in his chair like a sick man, with his eyes closed, his teeth clenched together. For, after all, he realized with a doubly stinging inwardness that it *was* because he wanted notoriety and praise that he had come to the mountains to live like a hermit.

Would a true hermit hire a cook? Would a true hermit lay five miles of telephone wire?

First, he wanted to throttle Mr. Mayo. Then he told himself in an agony that the boy would spread the scandal that he had scented out through the length and breadth of the mountains. Ah, but perhaps the bullet from the steady gun of the great Dean Thomas would put out that restless life before the tongue of Tommy had had time to utter a single syllable to listening ears.

Suddenly, Mr. Derby found himself truly praying for the death of another human being. He started to his feet with weakness in his soul. He who had been dispensing comfort for the souls of other men; he who had been spreading goodness through the mountains as one who spends from an inexhaustible store—he now struck a hand upon his forehead.

"God be merciful to me, a sinner!" said the Reverend Nicholas Derby.

In the meantime, Tommy had ridden with the horse of the minister no farther than the winding of the trail that carried them to the edge of the forest of the pine trees. There he paused long enough to tie the horse to a sapling by the reins. The storm was, after all, not a cold storm, and the horse could not be vitally injured before morning. In the meantime, his purpose was served. The minister, he felt, was successfully shut out of the picture, and Tommy could go on to play his hand alone—if it were not, by this time, much too late!

At that thought, he spoke to Hagan, and the great horse responded with the tireless force of an engine that drives on so long as there is fuel to feed it. And pride was like fuel in the heart of the stallion.

Presently, on that northward trail, the mountains rose in a black wall above them, vaguely crowned with rolling summits, like clouds. The trail seemed driving against a solid wall of rock. No, for now it turned a sudden corner and drove into a mist of darkness. He was in a narrow valley, shaped as though a great wedge had been hammered down through the center of the mountains.

There was a faint bubbling of water through the midst of the gorge. That small presence was the force which had gone through the earth and solid rock and made the ravine. Tommy thought of that, and smiled in his wonder. He raised his face to the gigantic sweep of clouds that brushed through the ravine, and he smiled again at the stars which twinkled for brief instants here and there in the sky.

He was very pleased. A tingling sense of luck and good fortune to come possessed him. Something winked through the trees at his right, like a star close to the horizon. He had gone on for a hundred yards before he remembered, with a start, that the horizon did not extend so low as to be visible through the trees at that point. There was nothing but the black face of the mountain here. What had made the light, then? The hand of man, of course, and there must be either a house or at least a fire somewhere among the trees.

He turned and rode back, eyeing the side of the road, carefully, and at last he found what he had more than half hoped for—an old road that turned in from the main trail. He could hardly call this new way, however, a road. There were two ruts, represented by streaks of grass. In the center, between what had been the ruts, there was now only a dense growth of tender young shrubbery, which must have cost at least some years for the growing—at this altitude.

Tommy dismounted and went ahead on foot. Hagan, following like a faithful dog, was warned farther back by a wave of the master's hand. They stole along a winding pathway for perhaps a hundred yards and then issued to the edge of a clearing. At least, it had at one time been a clearing.

Now it was like the old roadway—overcome with young shrubbery which was growing apace. In the midst of the clearing, the house was still standing. More than that, it was occupied—for the yellow of firelight was shaking across the windows, and now and again the shadow of a human head came like a blot against the gold of the light.

There were horses, too. From under the sheds at the rear of the house came a grunt and a sudden stamping as though one animal had made a lunge for another. This was too much for Hagan. Tommy knew what was about to happen when he heard the soft jingling of the bridle as the stallion threw up his head.

But he was too far away to get back in time to choke off the neigh. It came ringing and vibrant. It stormed and crashed like the blast of a hundred bugles in the ears of Tommy. He caught desperately at the nose of the big black. Then he waited.

He could not mount the horse and hastily retreat, unless he wished to give up all his hopes of spying upon the others this night. For the noise of his withdrawal would certainly be noted. He decided to remain where he was, and see what investigation would be made of the noise.

Almost at once, he saw a door opened and in a shaft of firelight, two men stepped out into the night.

25

They did not hesitate, but came straight toward him as though they saw him clear as day. Yet he did not see how the two men could make him out, close as he was, against the background of trees. As for them, he had them against the house, and enough light came from this to make them at least visible. Two hulking shadows, they approached within a short distance of him. It seemed to Tommy that he could almost make out the features of their faces, and surely they saw him.

"It wasn't this way," said one, halting.

"I heard it."

"So did I."

"If it didn't come from this direction, then I ain't got ears."

"Some that have got ears dunno how to use them."

"That'll do out of you. That whinny come from over in here somewheres."

"I say that it come from one of the hosses back in the shed."

"Right over in here somewhere—"

"How could a hoss come here?"

"That's what the Dean wants us to find out. I dunno how, but I want to find out where."

"You talk like a fool. That hoss yapped from back in the shed. Let's go back there, anyways, and see if any of them hosses is loose."

"That's more like sense than anything else you've said. We'll go back there and have a look."

They faded away in a few strides, and Tommy hastily moved into the trees with the black horse. There he left Hagan, near at hand from the house—if ever it were the luck of Tommy to come from that same house and to sit again upon the back of peerless Hagan. He himself went back near the place where he had originally paused with the stallion.

There, at the edge of the trees, he crouched down. He was cold now—miserably cold—because the action of riding had kept him only warm enough to avoid numbness. And now he was thoroughly weary, if, indeed, Tommy ever grew really tired.

At least, some of the freshness was gone from his strength, and he was more like other men. Presently the pair returned from the direction of the horse shed. They stopped, again, near the point where the old roadway verged on the clearing. Then the more aggressive of the pair advanced half a dozen strides into the darkness. When he paused he was within arm's reach of Tommy, as the latter crouched behind a tree.

The hunter stamped with impatience. "A fool place to stop in!" he exclaimed. "Why didn't we keep heading on—even if we had to ride all night? We could of made the town in another couple of hours, I think. It shouldn't be far from here."

"Because the Dean ain't set on getting with his wife to any town—not right away! He's set on keeping her off by herself, where he ain't gunna run so much chance of losing her right quick."

"We'll go back and tell him it was one of the hosses from the shed that must of hollered."

Back they went, and Tommy skulked behind them. When they entered by the door, he looked in through the window and saw a ragged room, the ceiling of which had fallen in and the floor of which was sagging. It sprang with a rotten weakness under the striding of the two young men. From another chamber a tall man with sand-colored hair and sand-colored eyes came out to meet them. Since half the panes were out of the window through which Tommy was peering, he could hear plainly.

The two made their report. They had searched everywhere; there was no sign of anything moving or living near the house, and their conclusion was that it must have been one of the horses from the shed which had neighed. The tall man listened gravely to them, and when he spoke his voice was gentle. Otherwise, every word would have been a stinging insult, to be instantly and fiercely resented.

"You haven't had time enough to search everywhere," he said. "None of the horses in that shed could have neighed like that. That was the neigh of a fresh horse. There was strength and go in the sound of that voice, and the nags in the shed are fagged out, every one of them. A neigh from one of them would sound like a groan, just now. That other fellow that we heard—his neigh sounded like a stallion's, to me. If you haven't found the horse, it shows that somebody has come up toward the house and hidden near it when he saw the place."

He made nothing of getting at the problem with this sort of reasoning, but Tommy, listening at the window, conceived a deep and lasting respect for this man. He knew it was Dean Thomas by the description of Harry Grant. And he saw at once that all that had been said about the Dean was not too much—or hardly enough!

For this big man had that sort of gentleness which seems to women to speak straight from a soft and kindly heart, and which men recognize at once as the voice of a purring tiger. The great Dean spoke softly because he kept over himself, at all times, the most perfect control.

But it was like looking at a smooth skin under which the muscles of power ripple and slide. So thought Tommy as he watched the face and form of this man and listened to his voice. Hearing Dean Thomas analyze so perfectly the situation outside the house, a sort of helplessness came over Tommy—a feeling that this stranger would be too much for him, under any circumstances.

At any rate, he did not wait for the three to come out as the first two hunters stood mute, while Dean went on: "We'll go out, all of us, and start hunting again. The pair of you turn to the right outside the door, and I'll turn to the left."

Tommy did not wait for them to come. He turned and ran like a greyhound for the place in the woods where he had secreted Hagan. On the verge of the forest, with the sharp tang of the wet pines in his nostrils, he turned and cast an anxious, longing glance behind him. There he paused—on the edge of safety, if he chose to put himself in the saddle on the fastest horse in the mountains—and there he balanced, on the edge of pleasure, also—that grim sort of pleasure which uses danger as a sauce to make life more palatable.

Certainly he had never in his life been so frightened as he was now—not even when Hagan had staggered and nearly fallen to destruction on the side of the cliff in crossing the shortcut through the mountains. For the Dean was more than a chasm; there was a poisonous certainty about the man that simply paralyzed resistance.

To compare great things with small, Tommy lingered on the edge of that clearing like the hypnotized bird which has seen the eyes of the snake hovering about her nest. And then he did what the terrified bird is supposed to do. He turned and hurried back into the clearing like a skulking beast, slipping along close to the edge of the trees, for, between him and the house, he could make out the forms of the hunters as they started out anew to search for him.

It seemed to Tommy most wonderful that this great man, the Dean, should have the girl unguarded in the house behind him, while he searched for enemies through the woods. Perhaps, after all, Dean Thomas was not invincible both in craft and in strength!

Straight through the clearing went both the couple and the

single hunter, as though they had decided before starting that the place to hunt for the intruder would be in the woods alone. As soon as they were out of view, Tommy was up and running low toward the house.

He hardly cared what part of it he reached. What he wanted was to be close under the wall so that the glow from window or broken door might not show him to the first observer. For something in the voices of all three of these men told him that they would not wait to ask questions; they would do their talking with voices of powder and lead.

His own guns were ready now. And when he got to the side of the house he dropped on both knees and leaned his weight against the wall to recover his breath. For danger is exhausting—and there had been danger enough during that day to have filled the cup of the bravest man that ever lived. Yet Tommy, as he leaned against the house, presently began to smile.

Here was the evening of the first day of his new life. Who could tell how many other days there would be like it? Well, let each man follow the course of his own desires, but for Tommy, he knew now that this was the sort of spice in the cup that he wanted!

When he had recovered a little, he stood up and began to go cautiously but swiftly around the house. For now, after all, was his priceless moment of opportunity. While the three searched through the woods for him, he could do something, perhaps, to reach the girl. After they returned—

Then another alternative—perhaps the most probable of all, suggested itself to Tommy and made him grit his teeth. Perhaps the great Dean, after all, had *not* left the house without leaving a guard over the girl. Some fourth man might be in there watching over her at this very moment.

Only exploration could tell that. He went on, like one walking a tightrope, suspended across a great waterfall. Turning the corner of the building, he went down the farther side. Then he heard within the house, and close to him, the rumble of a man's voice, answered quickly and lightly in the tones of a girl!

This was the worst expectation realized almost as soon as it had entered his mind. A little more, and he stood peering through a window into a chamber as rude as the first one which he had seen in the ruined house. There was a fire, however, blazing cheerfully on an open hearth, and there was a big fellow standing in front of the fire, and a girl nearby, lying on an improvised couch made of saddles and saddle blankets.

It was the girl of Harry Grant's photograph. But it was certain, in the mind of Tommy, that the picture had slandered her. Certainly her features were not classically regular, but she had an exquisitely clear, high color, and she seemed to Tommy, even after he had been watching her only a few moments, one of those girls who smile only when there is a cause for smiling.

She lay with her head in one arm, tired and resting, but with an apparent stock of energy dormant in her and waiting to be called upon in the case of an emergency.

"There *can't* be anyone hanging around in the woods in weather like this," Muriel Grant was saying.

"The Dean has a hunch," answered the big man, "and there's a saying among the boys that the Dean is never *all* wrong."

Here Tommy pressed close to the empty window, put his hand through the hole left by a broken pane, and beckoned boldly to the cowpuncher by the fire.

26

It was easy enough to do this unperceived, for the puncher faced the window and the girl was turned away. In response the man began to whistle softly and stroll toward the window, where he acted as though he were looking carelessly forth upon the darkness of the night.

"Break away," whispered Tommy, putting his face recklessly close to the glass and trusting to the dimness of the night to conceal him even when he was so near. "Break away and come out here!"

"Does the Dean want me?"

"Of course! There's news, old boy!"

The tall man went back to the fire and lingered there a moment. He stifled a yawn—but his eyes were as bright as polished steel.

"I'm so sleepy I got to take a breath of the outside air," said he. "I'll be back again in a minute or two."

"I'll go along," said the girl, sitting up, while Tommy's heart fell.

"You'll stay put, I guess," said the puncher, grinning back to her. "The Dean told me to keep you here."

"Am I a prisoner?" The girl smiled.

"You're Mrs. Dean Thomas now," answered the tall man, "and by a way of speaking I suppose that that means that you *are* a prisoner!"

She took it cheerfully enough and lay back on her manufactured couch again. "I'll promise not to stir."

The other left the room; Tommy drew a revolver and waited. He would have preferred to go to meet the other, to take the noise of the encounter away from the ears of the girl, but he could not tell from what direction the big man would come. When he heard him it was from the left, and Tommy was off in an instant to forestall him. Presently he saw a looming bulk before him.

"Now, Sammy, what does the chief want to—"

Then, in the middle of his sentence, rather by some warning instinct than anything he could possibly have seen, he appeared to guess at danger. He broke off with a gasp and reached for a gun.

There was no time for a swing of the revolver which Tommy carried in his right hand. There was barely space that allowed him to drive his left fist into the face of the stranger. A pugilist would have admired the uncanny accuracy with which that snapping punch was landed, just a shade to the right of the point of the victim's chin.

The pugilist would have understood why the knees of the big man drooped, and why, though his revolver was now out of the holster, it hung nerveless in his hand. He had no fraction of a second to recover, for the long barrel of a heavy Colt's revolver, made of refined steel, was laid along the side of his head. Down with a great sigh he went, like a very weary man!

Tommy went swiftly to work on him. He had never had practice in just such work before, but he had given much thought and invention to just such details as this little task, and he knew exactly what must be done and how to do it. It took him fewer seconds to tie the cowpuncher, hand and foot, than it takes an average range rider to throw and tie a yearling of even the most limp type. Then he gagged the victim thoroughly, but not murderously. When that was ended he stood up and hurried to the back of the house, from which direction the stunned man had come.

The door was open, and Tommy, in another instant, was at the door of the room in which the girl was waiting. He tapped and, hearing a faint exclamation within, pushed the door open.

"You must have been walking on feathers," she called cheerfully. "I didn't hear a—"

Then her eye recognized that the face was that of a stranger, and it went blank with fear. She was already sitting up, and now she did what any Western girl of the true range type must have thought of, no matter if few of them could have had the courage to execute their thoughts.

She tore a little .32-caliber revolver out of a red-morocco holster and held it with a firm grip in her hand, the muzzle resting on her knee, the barrel steady. Tommy knew there was no tremor by the firmness with which the highlight kept in place upon the steel.

"I don't know you," said Muriel Grant Thomas, with a little, savage flare of her nostrils. "Keep back by the door and put up your hands!"

He obeyed without a word, and he stood so quietly by the door and smiled so cheerfully upon her, that presently her fear seemed to abate, and a little color of shame passed over her face as she eyed his rags.

"You poor fellow!" said Muriel. "Have you been out in the storm like *that*?"

"Like this." Tommy smiled.

She did not exactly like that smile. It seemed good-natured and careless—but it seemed *too* good-natured and careless to be on the lips of a man who stood with his back against a door and his hands over his head—even though it were only a woman who held him up!

"It was your horse that neighed a little moment ago!" cried she.

"It was," he admitted.

"But why didn't you come right in?"

"I saw a pair of men come out with guns in their hands. That didn't look very hospitable, did it?"

"Of course not," she admitted. "What did you do with the horse?"

"I put him back in the woods and came on to see how things were."

"You kept the horse safe and took a risk for yourself?" she asked, smiling a little now.

For she began to see that he was young, as her excitement passed—very young, perhaps only in his early twenties. And, for some reason which the world can never expect to understand, women appear to feel that young men cannot be dangerous!

"I needed to have a means of getting away in a pinch," he explained.

"Only, I don't see how. I guess you can put your hands down. Heavens! Haven't you even a hat?"

"No."

"Through this—but did the wind blow it away?"

"It was knocked off in the brush—somewhere back along the shortcut."

"The shortcut!"

"Yes."

"You haven't crossed that!"

"Yes."

"But at night?"

"We had to."

"Why?"

"There was a woman—"

"Sick?"

"In pretty bad danger."

"You got help for her, then! And on the way back—"

"She can help herself, I suppose," he broke in.

There was something about this answer which made the girl stiffen with a touch of apprehension, and she frowned in a more concentrated survey of the young man. He did not seem so young, now; he might be as much as five years older than her first guess about him. He had a way of meeting her stare solidly and piercingly, so that when she opened her eyes to look at him, his own gaze slid down into her heart and found all sorts of unsuspected matter there. She was growing uncomfortable—frightfully uncomfortable.

"Tell me," said the girl, "how in the world you could have got into the house without meeting a man—"

"What sort of a man?"

"A big, tall fellow."

"I *did* meet him."

She parted her lips and then closed them again. She had seen, it seemed to her, a little glimmer of yellow light that appeared in the soft, brown eyes of the handsome youth. But the light went out at once. No doubt it was only the reflection of the gold of the liquid firelight which spilled across the floor and upon the time-stained walls so generously.

"You met him," she said, and the fear in her kept rising every moment. "But did he tell you that you could come in here?"

"I didn't ask him," said Tommy.

"You—"

"I didn't have time, really," said Tommy. "Because I thought he might not want to let me go by him. In fact, he reached for a gun almost before he had a chance to see my face."

He was very apologetic. But the girl wished that his hands were still above his head. It seemed to her, now, that there had been a mockery in the manner in which he had surrendered so easily to her.

"He reached for his gun!" she gasped. "But I didn't hear a sound of a squabble—just a faint murmur near the house— as though he were talking—to himself."

"He didn't finish speaking," confessed Tommy. "I had to knock him down and leave him tied and gagged there. You see, there wasn't time to persuade him. He wouldn't wait to be persuaded, Miss Grant."

She was standing, by this time, backing away from him,

and though she had a tight grip on the butt of the revolver, the muzzle of the gun was wobbling most shamefully as she strove to keep it pointed full upon the enemy. The faint smile, which she had noticed before, was upon his lips. She felt nothing but scorn, mockery, contempt, in his expression.

"Will you tell me who you are?" she asked. "I don't want to call; I don't want to make a noise with that gun. But I think I had better tell you that I am not Muriel Grant any longer."

"Oh?" said he politely.

"I am Muriel Thomas. My husband is Dean Thomas," said she desperately. "And he is outside—I can easily call Dean Thomas into this house!"

She spoke as though the power of a thunderbolt were at her command. But again it seemed to the girl that the young man's smile did not waver, and that into his brown eyes there came a faint touch of yellow light.

"I don't know about Dean Thomas," said he. "But I do know that you are the girl I came for."

"Do you mean what I hear you say?"

"You're the girl who is in trouble."

"I? I have just married Dean."

"Sometimes," said the youth, "we're in a lot of trouble without knowing it!"

27

The wind and the storm had fallen in violence, but they began with a sudden venom. A great gust of rain crashed against the roof of the house. The very weight of the falling water seemed to shake the building, and for a moment torrents must have been descending, for a leak formed in a corner of the room, and a noisy spout of water began to drop.

It increased the panic of Muriel Grant. For there is nothing destroys nerve poise so utterly as uncontrolled noise. She drew herself still farther from the stranger. Then, as the confused sound died away a little, she forced herself to smile in a breathless sort of way.

"I want to know your name," said she suddenly.

"My name is Tommy Mayo," said he.

She had heard that name before, and she changed color a little. In the beginning, she had felt that the very weight of the name of her husband should be enough to destroy the confidence of any other man. But here was one who, in spite of his youth, had built a formidable name for himself. She had heard the great Dean speak, that very day, with much respect of the young unknown who had met Morrissey and shot him down in the town of Newbury.

"You are *hunting* for Dean Thomas!" was her audible conclusion.

"There's nothing I want less than to meet him," said Tommy. "I promise you that!"

"I want to understand," said the girl. "I don't want to call for help!"

"Have I harmed you?"

"No. But you say that you have come for me."

"I have. But how can I *make* you come with me?"

"What brings you here, then?"

"To try to persuade you."

"You're not out of your wits," said the girl. "But why do you say such things? How can you persuade me?"

"If I can keep you here long enough, your father will be along to try what he can say to you."

"Dad is coming!" cried Muriel Grant Thomas. "He is coming? Heaven help me if he and the Dean come face to face!"

"You might have thought of that before you married Thomas," said the boy. "Of course your father would hunt for you."

"We've ridden like mad all the day. How could I dream that he would follow me? That he would be able to?"

"He lamed his horse in the shortcut."

"Did he ride that with you?" she cried.

"Yes. He made me go with him. He lamed his mare and then he tried to ride mine—but Hagan won't have two masters. Then I went on to do what I could, and your father is following after me. He may be here in a few hours!"

She was quite stunned by this news, and she pressed a hand against the wet wall behind her, as though Tommy were pressing her back with a physical force.

"I didn't know," she whispered, "that he cared so much about me! I never dreamed that he did!"

"Why?" asked Tommy. "Why didn't you dream it?"

He smiled at her—that queer, archaic smile which she could not understand—like the smile of the statue of some dead king of Egypt which seems, in turn, cruel, pathetic, or merely sphinxlike and strange—a smile which may be mere wonder or else too much knowledge! Muriel, watching this slender youth, was struck with awe.

It seemed to her, then, that he smiled in pity of the lack of understanding with which she had regarded her father; it seemed to her that there was scorn of her lack of comprehension, too, and suddenly she flushed with shame.

"How could I tell?" she gasped. "I was left in that horrible barn of a house with that dead-faced old woman to watch me like a fox, always watching me, day and night; just that old woman and the stained wallpaper and the books and the studies. How could I guess that he cared for me when he left me in such a place—and—and I never saw him except once a year, say? I never saw him. He was never tender. He treated me—how could I guess that he cared for me, Tommy Mayo?"

It began to seem to her, suddenly, as though the grounds for her defense had slipped away from her, and she was standing upon a foundation of sand—as though she had no defense at all. Besides, here was this strange young man with the archaic smile watching her silently. He understood, it seemed, and she understood not at all!

"I don't know how you could have guessed," said he. "Except that you might have known that it was hard for him to stay in one place."

She flushed again and stiffened. "I know. I know what manner of life he leads. I know that he—has no honest profession. That was another thing. I was living on stolen money—and when Dean Thomas came and offered me a home—"

Tommy Mayo did not know a great deal. But he felt that, if he were to accomplish anything, he would have to step now and again into the dark of surmise. He merely said:

"And is Dean Thomas going to support you with honest money?"

His inflection made it a stiletto stab that cut her to the

quick. And, beginning an answer to him, she found that her lips were moving, but that no sound came.

"Is he—" she said.

"I'll tell no stories," said Tommy Mayo. "But what does he call his profession?"

"A—rancher," whispered Muriel Grant.

"Who rides to get married with three men! Well, a queer sort of a peaceful rancher!"

She was silent, but wild surmises were rushing through her eyes.

"How long have you known him?"

"He came—oh, long ago. I always knew his name. But two days ago he came again. I was terribly frightened. I had always been taught to think of the Dean as a sort of monster. When I saw that he wasn't a monster—and he was so gentle. Then dad had told me so many wrong things about him."

"After all," said Tommy, "I suppose that your father ought to have some way of judging him. He ought to know the Dean, I guess. Weren't they partners in business together? But maybe that was an honest business!"

He smiled again, and the smile did more to her than his speech. She bit her lip, and the place where the teeth touched the flesh remained white for a long moment.

Then he said gravely: "I guess you married him because you were tired of your old life. But not because you loved him."

"I haven't said that."

"It's true, though."

She felt that he was turning upon her inward soul a light so penetrating and vital that she could not endure it for another moment—as though he were apt, at any moment, to force into her own sight things which she must not, things which she dared not, face and consider. She feared him with a mortal dread. There was no doubt, now, about the nature of his smile. It was the smile of knowledge which embraced a perfect estimate of her. He knew about her the very things which she did not know about herself.

While he talked, the figure of the Dean was transformed. He became, not the gentle-spoken fellow who had married her—who had swept her out of her old home and into the world in the circle of his arm. Reverting to an old picture, she saw him once more as he had been when she saw him only through the eyes of her father—a cold, relentless, overwise, mortal enemy. All of this floated dimly through her mind.

"I won't let you stay here another moment," whispered Muriel. "Because, if he comes back—"

"Oh," said Tommy, "I'm not going to leave you! Not at all! I'm here to stay until your father comes along."

"But Dean—"

"He'll wait outside," said Tommy, and still he smiled upon her. "When you get to thinking the whole thing over—I suppose you feel a little better about it, don't you—better about having him outside while he hunts for me?"

It was true. There was a vast relief in her heart. She did not want to confront her husband again. The door through which he had stepped into her heart was closed and bolted. She saw that she was looking at the cold truth about him—or what she now felt to be the truth. What she had done, in flying away from home with Dean Thomas, was to elope with the hope of a brighter life, rather than from love of any man.

"But," said Tommy, "if you want me to, I'll go outside and wait for the Dean there."

She did not answer, but turned her head toward the window. And it seemed to her that she found a sign of happier times there. For the great downpour of rain had been a clearing-up shower. The clouds had emptied themselves, and now the changing wind whipped the sky clean in no time. A broad moon was somewhere in the sky, and now its light began to silver outside the window. And the girl could look beyond to the dark-headed forest which was ranked there.

Tommy had turned and stepped toward the door of the room. "Shall I go out?"

"No!" she cried. "Oh, wait here with me. And when dad comes—ah, what a fool I have been!"

"Very well," said Tommy. "I'll secure the door a little, in the first place."

He took up two broken, half-rotted boards and propped them against it. Then he retired to a dark corner and took from his pocket a leather case. Presently she saw him join the sections of a flute, and now a thin trail of silver music floated through the room and passed out the window and was one with the moonlight which brooded there.

A sense of happiness increased in Tommy Mayo. Presently he was blowing his flute for the girl and for her only. He saw it take hold upon her and saw her head raised, courage in her eyes and resolution in her face. He founded, in that moment, the cornerstone of his solid hatred and scorn of women which was to grow to such a great fabric. That he, a stranger, should have stepped into that chamber and within such a few moments have changed the whole tenor of her thoughts!

For this must be known about Tommy, if one is to understand all the future of his strange life: that he could never see wherein he differed from other men. Not for many and many a day, at least. A time came when he was to know, but that is another story.

But there he sat, whistling his song without words, until a voice shouted suddenly from outside the house, and a stifled groan answered it.

28

It was big Dean Thomas who called, and it was the fallen, bound, and gagged man who made answer as the Dean tore the gag from his lips.

"What the devil?" cried the Dean. "What's done this? Where does that music come from? Has Muriel started to—"

There was a mumbling answer, and then a rapid fall of footsteps. Presently those footfalls entered the house, and a hand tried the door strongly.

"Muriel!" cried the voice of the Dean, raised in agony. "Are you there?"

"Yes."

"Thank heaven! Then tell me, by all that's wonderful, why the door is secured from the inside?"

Tommy listened with his head calmly cocked upon one side. By the question, and more by the tone of the voice of the Dean, he could tell well enough that, no matter from what motives of revenge the Dean had gone to marry the girl, there was only the motive of love remaining in his heart now!

Since Tommy had formed the habit of thinking to himself and expressing his thoughts in the blown phrases of the music from his flute, he blew from it now a plaintive trill of phrases which sounded very like an apt mockery of the Dean and his question outside the door.

"For heaven's sake!" cried the gunfighter. "Who is blowing that flute?"

"A friend," said Tommy, for emotion made the girl mute.

There was a gasp and then a violent effort which thrust the door open an inch or more and threatened to tear it from its hinges.

"What friend? What foolishness is this?" shouted the Dean.

All the affected smoothness was gone from his voice now. He was all lion as he raged outside the door.

"Steady," cautioned Tom. "I don't want to split that door in two with a bullet. But if you lay a hand on it again I'll have to turn my gun loose to talk for itself!"

There was a breath of silence, doubly long because it came from such a man as the Dean, and at such a time.

"Muriel," said he at last. "I'm horribly frightened. I know that it can't be anything but a jest. But will you please speak to me for yourself?"

She was standing near the fire so that Tommy could watch her face and see her waver like the flame of the fire itself. He smiled at this evidence of pain, a very cruel smile in so young a man.

But she answered with a voice strangely strong and steady: "Dean, I've been thinking of things that I haven't had time to think about in the last two days."

"Tell me! Tell me!" he pleaded.

"Things that weren't in my head before. Doubts about you, Dean."

He groaned. "Tell me what they are!"

"You called yourself a rancher, Dean."

"I have a ranch—I swear!"

Now, Tommy felt no particular emotion, at this moment, except one of great insecurity so far as his scalp was concerned, but he forced his voice to ring out harshly:

"You lie! Tell the lady how many acres are in that farm of yours!"

Then he waited, half shocked at his own impertinent suggestion—but with a growing incredulity and joy, as the half seconds fled and still Mr. Dean Thomas had not made any answer.

"Dean," cried the girl, "will you answer?"

"Or be hanged," suggested Tommy, and then, by a sheer bubbling over of the devil which was in him, he broke into a hearty laughter.

The answer of the Dean was a savage snarl, most like the voice of a wild beast: "Shall I answer such questions from my own wife, when there's a strange man in the room with her? Muriel, have you gone mad? Do you doubt that I have money?"

"Stolen money is dirty money to her," said Tommy, "and she doesn't like the things it buys."

"Who are you?" thundered Dean Thomas.

"My name is Tommy Mayo."

"That tallies with the black horse and the saddle, then! You young fool, you've lost your horse and your saddle. Do you want to throw away your head, too, tonight?"

"My head feels pretty safe."

"Mayo, you know that there are four of us!"

"I know that."

"Can you match us?"

"I have reenforcements coming."

"What? That is an old story. I tell you, Tommy Mayo, that unless you open the door and come out, I'll smash it down. But if you come out, I'll let you go away safe. If you have to be forced out, you may not leave the house alive!"

"Dean!" cried the girl.

"I hear you, Muriel!" said the Dean sullenly. "But what else can I do? It's the only way."

"You see," said Tommy to her, "that there's a little bit of the beast in your husband! I hope tonight doesn't make you a widow!"

He approached the door.

"You shall not go!" whispered the girl, clinging to his arm. "He means murder! There's nothing that he will stop at. I read it in his voice, and I remember everything that dad has told me about him! It was true, and I was a fool to come with him!"

"Listen to me," said Tommy. "I am going to talk quietly, but I shall have to talk out of your hearing. I promise that there will be no shooting through the door. Will you go back to the farther corner of the room?"

She obeyed in silence, as though realizing that she could not hope to control him. There she cowered while Tommy stood beside the door.

"Well, Dean?" he said crisply.

"Well?" answered the big man outside the room.

"Talk softly. I think that neither of us wants her to overhear what we're saying."

"Right. Now tell me what the devil you—"

"The jig is up for you. I came on ahead to see what I could do. But it only needed a touch. When I found her five minutes was enough. You found my horse while I was finding the truth about you for her. The best thing that you can do, to make a favorable impression on her, is to say a polite good-bye to her and ride away. Do you understand?"

The Dean laughed darkly. "And leave you here with her?" he asked savagely.

"And leave me here with her. Otherwise, I'll stay on here until tomorrow morning. And her father will be here before dawn."

"He will not be fool enough."

"You don't know him, Dean."

"I know he's too much of a fox to put his head in a trap."

"He was fool enough to try to cross the shortcut by night, and in a storm. Oh, he'll come here and make some attempt against you, my friend. And when you kill him, well, you will cut your throat with his daughter."

"I am to stay here and fold my arms and give up?"

"What else is there left to do? The harder you fight to get her, the more perfectly you will be sure to alienate her."

He paused, and in the pause he could hear the heavy breathing of the big man beyond the door.

"I'll tear the door down and have you, Mayo!"

"You'll have a dozen chunks of lead through your head before you get in."

"We can break down the door with a swung log, and you know it. You young fool, do you think that you could stop the rush of four of us? We're none of us weaklings."

"Partner, I can try. It won't do, Dean. If the four of you try to get through the doorway, at least two of you will die. And even if you are one of the two lucky ones, do you think that the girl will ever forget this room dyed in crimson?"

"Curse you, I know all of that. But have her I must and I shall. I'll never sit down and give her up."

Tommy knew that he meant what he said.

After all, there was no romantic joy in his heart at the thought of giving up his life in the defense of a girl like this. Yet there was a gigantic leap of the heart at the thought of confronting the Dean face to face—terror and joy commingled!

He thought of an alternative and proposed it.

"There's another way, Dean," said he, "if you'll stand to me face to face."

"I?" cried the Dean. "I? Stand to you—or any other man? Yes!" His voice fairly shook with his joy.

"There's a gap through the trees to the east," said Tommy. "I can look through the window down that gap and away over the hilltop, beyond. Well, Dean, when I see three men go one by one over the top of that hill and disappear—then I'll come out and meet you. Do you agree to that?"

"Mayo, do you mean it?"

"I mean it."

"Will you swear that you'll play square?"

"Yes," said Tommy.

"Then—it's done! Watch the hill. Kid, I'm going to trust

you. I'll send the three away. Then I'll wait on the edge of the trees. Only tell me first, how did you trail me here?''

''By luck,'' said Tommy.

''Kid, it wasn't luck that brought you here tonight—it was a bad break for you! You'll find that out when you take your chance with me.''

Suddenly his footstep was heard retreating down the hall, and Tommy turned back to the girl.

''I've brought him to reason,'' he said with an assumed triumph. ''He's had to see, at last, that he can't win anything from us by force. Now he has agreed to send off his three men. After that I'm to meet him outside and we'll discuss terms without guns! That will decide the issue.''

''Do you mean that?''

''I do.''

''Will you swear that there is no danger to you?''

''None in the world,'' vowed the perjurer.

''It doesn't seem possible. But then—I think that you could do what other men could not.''

29

One by one, three dim silhouettes appeared against the eastern sky and its pale flood of moonshine. And then they went out over the top of the hill. At that moment Tommy took the hand of the girl in his own.

"Wish me luck," said Tommy cheerfully.

"With all my heart!" said she.

And so Tommy went out to meet his fate for the second time that day—that long, wild day!

For it was not yet midnight, and the moon hung exactly in the zenith, shedding a bright light over the forest—a light more brilliant than any can realize saving those who have seen the moon at her best in the thin air of the mountain desert. He passed with his light, quick step down the hallway of the house and through the backyard and out the side gate and so, at the farther corner of the house, he paused again and searched the edges of the trees.

There he saw the other waiting, and immediately the tall form of the Dean stepped out from the trees with a raised hand, as though at once in greeting and in invitation. Tommy walked out in perfect confidence to meet the other.

They were much too distant, in such a light as this, for any accuracy in revolver shooting, and so it was that he went with his head high, careless, when a blow was struck him from the side. A burning pang thrust through his body, and, as he fell to the earth, the crash of the rifle explosion sounded in his ears, followed, as he lay on the ground, by the clangor of dim echoes that died slowly away.

He knew that he was struck to the verge of death, or death itself. All his lower body was numb. Only his arms and his head were free to move. And instinctively, as he fell, a revolver had come into each of his hands.

How had it happened? Not at the hand of the tall man, certainly. For big Dean Thomas had been walking straight toward him, and this blow had come from the side. The explanation shot easily through his mind: Of the three silhouettes of horsemen which he had seen against the eastern sky, only two were real.

The other, no doubt, was the coat and the hat of a man stuffed with brush and strapped in place. Yes, as he lay flat on his back, he saw a man, coatless and hatless, the rifle in his hand, leap out from the trees with a shout of triumph. From the house behind Tommy, he heard a wailing scream of terror and grief. That cry went like a needlepoint through his mind, and he forgot all other pain.

It was very simple. He had only to turn his head a trifle, and his eye came in line with the barrel of the revolver which lay thrown out at the full stretch of his arm upon the ground. He had only to turn his head and let the coatless murderer run into the field of the sight. Then he pulled the trigger, and the other pitched with a yell upon his face.

A high, weird scream, that was, and it died in the midst of its utterance as the man's soul leaped from his parted lips. There was an answering shout, and a bullet smashed into Tommy's right thigh.

He lifted his head and saw Dean Thomas paused, with a gun in either hand, making sharp target practice at the fallen enemy. Tommy tried a snapshot back, and the hat was flicked from the head of Thomas. His long hair blew back, flashing in the moonshine. He fired again, and another thrilling hand of fire caught the heart of Tommy and wrung it.

There was only an instant of fire-seared consciousness left to him, and he used it to lift himself on his left elbow and sent a 45-caliber slug through the head of Dean Thomas—a neatly placed bullet that took the Dean fairly between the eyes and ushered him out of this world.

Tommy did not even see the tall man fall, for the instant that his finger launched the bullet darkness covered him gently and closed out the agony from his inner mind.

This is the truth of how Tommy Mayo began his career. Some people tell the story with many more marvels attached. That was because they knew what Tommy did in his later days. But, at that time, it was quite enough for him to have faced one Dean Thomas and another murderous rascal besides. Also, Tommy was not then the half of what he afterward became.

Even so, take it all in all, in this single day of his life he crammed the hint and the promise of all that he was afterward to become. Whether there was more good or bad in him, each reader must decide for himself. We who record the history cannot tell.

One bit of direct criticism can be taken from the lips of Mr. Harry Grant, spoken by him some two months later as he and Muriel Grant sat on the veranda of his solemn old house in the mountains and watched Tommy, fortified with his newly recovered strength, riding upon the black stallion, back and forth, back and forth, through the clearing beneath the house from the forest on one side to the forest on the other side. Eventually, he turned the black horse among the trees and was lost to view.

"Where has he gone?" asked Muriel curiously, but in a weary voice that all but trembled with fatigue.

For she was not yet all recovered from that strain of nursing Tommy which had worn her out, week after weary week, following the fight by night which had made her a widow before she had well become a wife.

"Perhaps he has gone for good," said Mr. Grant. "There was a queer glint in his eye as he sat by the open window, last night. You can't tell. He may be off following the devil around a corner of the world."

"Do you mean that?" asked Muriel.

Her voice trembled so much that Mr. Grant bit his lip and was glad that the darkness hid his expression from her eyes.

"I mean that," he declared. And then he added with a savage earnestness: "I begin to hope that he *has* gone for good! Because, Muriel, I'm afraid that you're taking him a little too seriously!"

He heard her gasp, but that was all.

"Because," said he, continuing, "it is all very well for men to take this rascal just as seriously as they please, but it is the height of folly for women to ever think of him twice. He's no good for them."

"Will you tell me why?" asked Muriel.

"I'll tell you," said Harry Grant. "A woman must have a man who will stay in one place for her own happiness. Tommy will never stay put. There is always something on the other side of the mountain, for him. He'll keep traveling until he finds it."

"What is it?" she asked.

"Oh, as for that, I suppose that Tommy himself doesn't quite know. But he has to go. The great good time is always coming and never here—for him. Except when he's fighting, I suppose!"

"That's not true!" said Muriel. "For a gentler and—"

"Tush!" said Grant. "How can a child talk about the devil and his affairs?"

This was rather blunt talk. At least, Mr. Grant was right in some degree. To be sure, he had many reasons for being grateful to Tommy, for the boy it was who, at the cost of three dreadful wounds and danger of his life, had removed from the path of Grant the great standing menace which was tormenting his existence.

No matter how great was the malice which the members of the old gang held against Grant, when they learned that he had for an ally a man who slew both the great Dean and another in one battle, they gave up their manhunt and let O'Neil lie in his grave unavenged.

For these things Grant should have been grateful. But he could not help uttering what he himself felt to be the truth. And, after all, he turned out a true prophet, for Tommy never came back from the forest, never again rode into the clearing.